He's Mr. Sensitivity!

"Maybe Jennifer doesn't want a macho guy like Mitch. Maybe she wants a *sensitive* guy instead."

"Like you."

"Hey, I can do sensitive."

"Oh yeah. You're a regular Mr. Sensitivity."

"Right. And that's why you and I are going to take Baby-sitting and Child Care 101."

Lucas stopped in his tracks. "You and I?" he said.

"You and I. Best buddies. Pals. Friends to the end."

"Wait a minute, Nick. . . ."

"Blood brothers, remember? Second grade? Don't forget the pledge we made."

"I haven't," he said. "I pledged to pull you out of quicksand, and you pledged to rescue me from shark-infested waters. Not a word about baby-sitting, Nick."

"*Please*, Lucas! I can't be the only boy in the class. Come on, you've got to help me out here. Do this one thing for me, and you'll never have to worry about shark-infested waters again."

The New Nick Kramer

OR

My Life as a Baby-sitter

JAMES HOWE

HYPERION PAPERBACKS FOR CHILDREN

New York

To Adam Carver
—J.H.

First Hyperion Paperback edition 1997
Text ©1995 by James Howe.

A hardcover edition of *The New Nick Kramer, or My Life as a Baby-sitter* is available from Hyperion Books for Children.

Printed in the United States of America.

1 3 5 7 9 10 8 6 4 2

The text for this book is set in 12-point Cheltenham.

Library of Congress Cataloging-in-Publication Data
Howe, James
The New Nick Kramer, or My life as a baby-sitter / James Howe—1st ed.
p.   cm.
Summary: Fourteen-year-old Nick signs up for a baby-sitting and child-care class to be near a beautiful new girl at school, but at first his attempts at real baby-sitting prove to be less than successful.
ISBN 0-7868-0066-6 (trade)—ISBN 0-7868-2053-5 (lib. bdg.)—ISBN 0-7868-1017-3 (pbk.)
[1. Babysitters—Fiction. 2. High schools—Fiction. 3. Schools—Fiction.]
I. Title.
PZ7.H8372My 1995
[Fic]—dc20
95-2148

Reprinted by arrangement with Hyperion Books for Children.

Contents

Chapter 1:

The New Nick Kramer

Looking back at the start of my freshman year, I had no plans to become a major baby-sitter. I mean, I had enough to worry about. High school. Girls. Basketball. Zits. Mitch Buckley. But sometimes things happen. And sometimes they happen for some pretty weird reasons.

Did I mention Mitch Buckley? Mitch Buckley was weird reason number one.

Mitch and I have known each other our whole lives, and as far back as I can remember there's been this *thing* between the two of us. What am I saying? Even *before* I can remember, there's been this thing between the two of us. My mom has this movie of when I was about one year old and Mitch and I were learning to walk. There's Mitch with his pudgy little legs and me with my knobby little knees, and there's my mom in the background going, "Come on, Nicky, you can do it." And there's his mom going, "That a boy,

Mitch." And there we are, wobbling our w_y to join the other upright homo sapiens. And—this happened, I swear, I've watched it maybe a hundred times—just as I'm about to reach my mother's loving arms, Mitch sticks out his foot and trips me! Lucky for me my mom had fast reflexes.

It was bad enough when it was just baby stuff. But by the time we got to school, forget it. I couldn't do anything without Mitch doing it better, couldn't go anywhere without Mitch getting there first.

Take that basketball game in seventh grade. It wasn't a big game or anything, but it was important to me because my dad was there. I wanted to show him what I could do. The score was tied, fourth quarter, forty seconds of play, and I had the ball. I was ready to nail the winning points, and then, I don't know what happened, I tripped on my shoelace or something. I didn't fall, I didn't even lose control of the ball, but the next thing I know Mitch is buzzing in my ear, "Nyah, nice going, Kramer." He gets the ball away from me, takes off, shoots, and *bull's-eye*! The buzzer sounds. The crowd goes wild. I get a pat on the back from my dad, and Mitch gets most valuable player.

Last spring was almost as bad. He didn't steal the ball this time; he stole the one and only girlfriend I ever had in my whole life. Okay, maybe she wasn't exactly my girlfriend. There was this girl, see, her name was Julianne Barberetto, and I'd been following her around all year. I didn't think she noticed me, but my friend Lucas Lubowski said the only way I could have been more obvious was to handcuff myself to her ankle. Anyway, three weeks before school ended, I got up the nerve to ask her to the big eighth-grade dance.

Guess what she said. "Sorry, I'm going with Mitch Buckley." He didn't even like Julianne! He just asked her so I couldn't.

After that, I decided I needed to get serious and put Mitch in his place once and for all. I gave this a lot of thought, and I didn't tell anyone. Not Lucas. Not my other friends. Not my mother. Especially not my mother. Oh, I did tell Pooch, that's my cat who thinks he's a dog, but I tell Pooch everything.

"Pooch," I said, when he jumped up on my bed one night and settled in on my chest (this makes sleeping difficult, but with a devoted pet like Pooch, you have to make sacrifices sometimes), "I'm going to beat Mitch at his own game."

This was not going to be easy. After all, the cards were seriously stacked in his favor. Mitch has what my mother describes as movie-star looks. Which, believe me, he knows. He's also a totally cool dresser and the best all-around athlete in our school. I've spent half my life wanting to *be* Mitch, and the other half trying to get him to move. When I was nine, I wrote his parents a letter pretending to be a movie producer who wanted Mitch to come to Hollywood. His parents didn't fall for it. I don't know why I thought it would work; I'm a lousy typist.

I've had to face the fact that Mitch isn't moving anywhere. He did go away for the summer, though, which not only gave me the chance to think of a plan but to put it into action. Which is why I spent my summer vacation working out. When I wasn't working out, I was mowing lawns so I could buy a whole new wardrobe. Then, just before school started, I got this amazing haircut. I was going to get my ear pierced, but my mother said not in her lifetime, and that was the end of the discussion. Lucas didn't pay much attention to my new look, but that's okay. He gets his clothes at the thrift store and puts them together in what my mother calls outfits. She likes Lucas. She says he amuses her. I'll bet if he got *his* ear pierced she'd think it was cute.

He did notice my new muscles, though, after I shoved my biceps in his face a few times. His exact words were, "Gee, Nicky Schwarzenegger." I think he meant it as a compliment. I'm not always sure with Lucas.

"So," he said as we were walking to school that first day of ninth grade, "who's it going to be?"

"Who's what going to be?" I kept checking out of

the sides of my eyes to see if anyone was noticing how cool I looked. The woman who lives at the end of my block gave me a strange look, but she gives everybody strange looks, and I think that has more to do with her than the people she's looking at.

"Who's going to be the lucky girl to win the new Nick Kramer as her door prize?" Lucas asked. I blushed, which I hated because that is something the old Nick Kramer would do. What can I tell you? I was still working on the new me; I didn't have all the bugs out yet.

I didn't answer right away. Not that I hadn't given it a lot of thought. Ever since Lucas had gone away to music camp for the summer, I'd had these nightly conversations with Pooch on the subject of women. After all, getting a girlfriend was an important part of my plan if I was going to outmacho Mitch. The problem was that after two months of thinking about it, I still hadn't come up with an answer.

"How do I know until I see who's around?" I said to Lucas at last.

"Nick, we've been going to school with the same girls for a hundred years."

"This is true," I admitted. Other than Julianne Barberetto, there wasn't anybody who interested me— and Julianne had moved away over the summer.

"What about Lindsay Donovan?" he asked.

"She's got an attitude."

"Michelle Fisher?"

"We've known each other since we went to nursery school together."

Lucas grabbed my shoulders. "Nick," he said, looking me straight in the eyes, "this is a small town. A *very* small town. We *all* went to nursery school together."

Instant depression. What good was it being the new Nick Kramer if everyone else was old? By the time we got to school, I was totally bummed.

Naturally, it was at the moment of my greatest self-doubt that I saw Mitch. He was leaning against a row of lockers, looking the way he always does, only better. He was with his buddy Augie Burger, a jock with a buzz cut and an IQ lower than his arches. Mitch glanced our way. My stomach began to hurt.

"This is it," I said to Lucas. "Showdown time."

Lucas hitched up his pants and pretended to spit a wad of tobacco out of the side of his mouth. "Whatever you say, pardner," he drawled.

I started toward Mitch and Augie. With every step I took, my stomach hurt a little more. I tried to convince myself that the reason for this was my washboard abs, but then I remembered I didn't have washboard abs. The truth probably had more to do with butterflies in my tummy.

Mitch and I locked stares until we were maybe

two feet apart. Then his eyes did a trigger-quick shift to Lucas.

"So, Lubowski," he said, "what's happening?"

"Oh, uh, nothing," Lucas replied. "Have a good summer, Mitch?"

"I always have a good summer, Lubowski."

I cleared my throat.

"Nicky," Mitch said, as if he'd just noticed I was there. I hate it when he calls me Nicky.

I smirked, just the way I'd been practicing in the mirror. "For a minute there, I thought you didn't recognize me," I said, holding out hope it was true. I *did* look pretty cool. Even Mitch would have to notice.

"Why wouldn't I recognize you?" he asked. "So, you going out for basketball this year?"

I held on to my smirk like a lifeline. "If I can fit it in."

Mitch smirked back. His smirk was better than mine. But then, he'd had a lot more practice. "Fit it into what?" he asked. "It's not exactly like you have a social life." Just what I'd been waiting for. A put-down from Mitch. But this time I was ready with the perfect comeback. "Oh, yeah?" I said. "Takes one to know one." Somehow, that hadn't come out the way I intended.

Augie laughed. Lucas and I call it his duh laugh. He gets this look like he knows he's supposed to be laughing, but he's not exactly sure why. Which, come to think of it, is sort of how Augie lives his whole life. Anyway, Mitch laughed, too, then started to say something, but the words never came out.

There, coming down the hall between Lindsay Donovan and Michelle Fisher, was the most beautiful girl ever to walk the corridors of Calvin Coolidge High. I mean, Lindsay and Michelle are okay. I guess you could even say they're pretty. But this girl was in a whole new league. It wasn't just her looks, which were drop-dead gorgeous; it was the way she walked. And the way she smiled. Right at me.

I blinked. My heart started pounding. My palms felt like sponges. I couldn't believe this was happening to me.

We watched the girls pass. Lindsay and Michelle said hi. The new girl smiled again. Smiles like that have started wars. This one was about to.

After they were out of earshot, Augie said, "Wow, wow, wow! Who's the babe?"

"Collect your eyeballs, Burger," Mitch said. "She was smiling at me."

"She wasn't smiling at you," I said. "She was looking right at me."

"Hardy, har," said Augie. "Don't make me laugh."

Mitch smirked again. "Really."

This was my chance. "And I say she was smiling at me, Mitch. What are you going to do about it?" I could hardly believe these words were coming out of my mouth. Now *this* was more like the new Nick Kramer!

"I'll tell you what I'm going to do about it, Nicky boy. I'm going to make you a little bet. I'll bet that I get a date with her before you do."

"That's too easy," I said, rising to the challenge. "I'll bet that she asks me to the Vice-Versa Dance. Me and *not* you, Buckley."

"You mean where the girls ask the boys? You're on."

We shook on it as Lucas whispered in my ear, "The new Nick Kramer is even dumber than the old one."

"One condition," I told Mitch. "Neither of us asks her out on a date. We have to wait for her to do the asking."

"No sweat," Mitch said. "So I get to go . . . I mean, the winner gets to go to the dance with this hot babe. What about the loser?"

"The loser gets to dance alone," I said, thinking fast. "At the first basketball game of the season. At halftime. Out on the court. Wearing a tutu." Brilliant.

"Are you crazy?" Lucas asked, his voice cracking. I made a mental note to have a little talk with Lucas about how best friends are supposed to back you up and not ask you if you're crazy in public.

"You're nuts," Augie chimed in. "Anyway, what's a tutu?"

"One less than a three-three," Lucas joked. Augie scratched his head.

Mitch hadn't said anything. Finally, he stuck out his hand. "Oh, Nicky," he said, "you're going to look so cute in a tutu."

I took his hand and shook it. "We'll see who looks cute," I told him.

The homeroom bell rang. "You've really done it this time," Lucas said as we walked away. "There're only five weeks until the dance. How are you going to get near this girl?"

"Lucas, my boy," I said, "where there's a will, there's a—"

A piece of paper landed at my feet. It had fluttered from the new girl's notebook as she passed. It was as if it had been faxed there by the gods of love. I picked it up. It was her schedule. A quick scan gave me the answer to my problem.

"There's a way," I said to Lucas as I took off down the hall.

"Jennifer!" I called out. The new girl turned and gave me a puzzled look.

I handed her the class schedule. "You're new here, right? Jennifer Edwards? I'm Nick Kramer. We're going to be seeing a lot of each other."

"Oh?"

"Yeah," I said, trying to sound manly or at least to

keep my voice from cracking. "I'll see you tomorrow in fifth period." I still had an open elective. Perfect.

She glanced at her schedule, then up at me. Her eyes opened wide. "Oh?" she said again. She may not have been a woman of many words, but the way she said them! I nodded and moved quickly toward my homeroom, trying to beat the late bell. Oh, yeah, I thought, we'll be seeing a lot of each other, all right—in Baby-sitting and Child Care 101.

Chapter 2:

Hey, I Can Do Sensitive

Today's Woman
What Do Women Want?

There's a lot being written these days about what women are looking for in a man. Does today's woman want the same kind of man her mother married? Is she Lois Lane trying to decide between Clark Kent and Superman? Or is she looking for an equal partner? Most of the women we talked to summed it up in one word: *sensitivity*.

Yes, today's women are still looking for men who aren't afraid of their sensitive side, men who can cradle a baby as easily as they cradle a football.

Lucas looked up from the magazine I'd handed him on the way to school the next morning.

"What does this have to do with life as we know it?" he asked.

"I can sum it up in one word," I told him. "Jennifer."

"She sells magazine subscriptions? What, you couldn't say no?"

"I told you yesterday, bubble brain. She's taking this baby-sitting class."

"Good for her. I still don't understand—"

"So I got to thinking."

Lucas groaned. "I hate when you do that," he said.

"Maybe Jennifer doesn't want a macho guy like Mitch. Maybe she wants a *sensitive* guy instead."

"Like you."

"Hey, I can do sensitive."

"Oh yeah. You're a regular Mr. Sensitivity."

"Right. And that's why you and I are going to take Baby-sitting and Child Care 101."

Lucas stopped in his tracks. "You and I?" he said.

"You and I. Best buddies. Pals. Friends to the end."

"Wait a minute, Nick. . . ."

"Blood brothers, remember? Second grade? Don't forget the pledge we made."

"I haven't," he said. "I pledged to pull you out of quicksand, and you pledged to rescue me from shark-infested waters. Not a word about baby-sitting, Nick."

I hated to do it, but desperation was setting in. I begged.

"*Please*, Lucas! I can't be the only boy in the class. Come on, you've got to help me out here. Do this one thing for me, and you'll never have to worry about shark-infested waters again."

Lucas shook his head. "You're pathetic," he said. "Okay, I'll do it."

"It's a great way to impress girls," I went on.

"I said I'll do it. But only because you're my friend. I don't care about girls. I have my harmonica."

I had no idea what one thing had to do with the other, but with Lucas I've learned not to ask. "Thanks, buddy," I said, punching his shoulder.

He rolled his eyes. "Come on, *pal*," he said. "We don't want to be late for diaper-changing class."

I'll admit it was weird being in a class with all girls—except for Lucas, of course. I really did owe him. The thing about Lucas is, he'd never remind me. Even if we *were* in shark-infested waters, he wouldn't say, "Nick, remember ninth grade? Baby-sitting class? It's time to pay up." That's the kind of person Lucas is. I'm lucky he's my friend.

As we were waiting for baby-sitting class to start, I wasn't sure he was feeling as grateful for my friendship as I was for his. He kept looking around as if he didn't know where he was. I shared the feeling, but pretended everything was okay.

"Lot of girls here," I said. "Cool, huh?"

Lucas nodded slowly. "Keen," he said. "Neat-o.

The best. How will I ever repay you? And not serve prison time, I mean."

"Aw, come on, Lucas, it won't be so bad. If Jennifer would just show up . . ." I couldn't understand it. The bell was about to ring, and no Jennifer. What if she'd changed her mind? What if I was stuck in this class all semester and Jennifer wasn't even taking it? My mind was racing with what-ifs when the bell rang, the teacher came in, and the door was shut.

Lucas grabbed my arm. "If Jennifer doesn't show," he said under his breath, "you're dead meat."

Luckily, the door opened at that moment, and Michelle, clutching her books and catching her breath, pulled Jennifer into the room. "Sorry," Michelle said. "We went to the wrong classroom."

"That's all right," Ms. Marlowe said. I knew that was her name because she'd just written it on the board. "Why don't you take those two empty seats next to . . ." She looked at me and smiled.

"Nick," I said. "Nick Kramer."

"Next to Nick."

Amazing. Not only were we in the same class, but Jennifer was sitting right next to me. She was wearing this incredible perfume or something. I thought I was going to faint.

"Hi," I said, doing this cool thing with my eyebrows. I knew it was cool because I'd practiced it in the mirror about a million times over the summer.

"Is something wrong?" Jennifer asked me.

"Wrong? Who, what, me? No. I just . . . you smell great. Like flowers. Like a garden. Like a big garden full of flowers."

"Too much fertilizer kills the flowers," Lucas whispered.

I ignored him. Jennifer smiled. "That's really sweet," she told me.

Eat your heart out, Mitch Buckley.

Ms. Marlowe began by asking each of us to introduce ourselves and tell why we were taking the class. Fortunately, I was in the middle of the first row so I had time to find just the right words. After all, this was going to be my opening shot at showing Jennifer that I was the perfect guy for her. The perfect *sensitive* guy.

"I'm Michelle Fisher," I heard Michelle saying. It was almost my turn. "I come from a large family and I've always loved kids. I guess that's why I'm taking the class. I want to be a better baby-sitter and know how to be a good mom myself someday."

"Excellent," Ms. Marlowe said. "And next we have . . ."

Jennifer let out this big sigh. "I'm Jennifer Edwards," she said, twirling her hair. She stared blankly ahead.

"Yes?" Ms. Marlowe said, prompting her.

"AndIdon'tknowwhyI'mtakingthisclass." The

words came out in rush. When she was finished, Jennifer looked up at Ms. Marlowe and smiled sweetly.

Ms. Marlowe raised her eyebrows as if she wasn't sure what to say. "Ah. Well. Perhaps you'll find your reason as you go along."

"Anything's possible," Jennifer said.

I was a little embarrassed for her, but then it occurred to me that maybe, just maybe, the reason she was taking the class was to meet a sensitive guy like me. Naturally, she wasn't going to say *that* to Ms. Marlowe.

"My name is Nick Kramer," I announced in a loud, clear voice. "And I'm taking this class because . . . well, you know how most boys want to grow up and become firemen or ballplayers or something like that? Not me. I've always wanted to be a dad."

Talk about an attention getter. Everybody was looking right at me, even Jennifer. "Oh yeah, I've had this thing about kids ever since *I* was one. I always thought they were the greatest things since, like, bread, and they've always taken to me, too, you know, the way birds and animals took to that saint, what's his name, Francis of A-sissy."

Everybody laughed, I wasn't sure why. I just kept going.

"So I figured I'm a natural, you know, to be a baby-sitter and all. And I'll probably learn good stuff here to help me be a *sensitive* dad when I'm older." I paused. Ms. Marlowe was staring at me. I remembered a word from that article I'd read. "A *nurturing* dad."

"Excuse me?" Ms. Marlowe said.

"I want to be a nurturing dad, nurturing my children like no man has nurtured before." Great line, I thought. I should be a writer.

I glanced at Jennifer. I could tell she was really impressed because she was staring at me. And for the first time all period she wasn't playing with her hair.

"Thank you, Nick," Ms. Marlowe said, "for . . . sharing that with us."

She turned to Lucas, who was still looking at me, his mouth hanging open.

"I'm Lucas Lubowski," he said slowly. "Why am I taking this class? Would you buy temporary insanity?"

To my surprise, Ms. Marlowe thought this was funny. I don't know what it is about Lucas. Everybody likes the guy. He can get away with murder.

After the rest of the class said pretty much the same stuff (nobody was as original as I was, believe me), Ms. Marlowe started passing out some papers. "In addition to what goes on in the classroom," she said, "each of you will be expected to fulfill thirty hours of baby-sitting time with the child or children of your choice. Here are some tips on how to get started, as well as a chart to keep track of your time."

That's when it hit me. Baby-sitting? Kids? *Thirty*

hours? I'm an only child. I'd never baby-sat in my life. Everything I'd said had been to impress Jennifer. I wasn't sure I even *liked* kids.

"Do we have to?" I said.

"Sorry, Nick," Ms. Marlowe said. "Did you say something?"

I hadn't meant to; the words had just come out. "Oh, uh, no. I mean, I said, do we have to . . . do only thirty hours? Can't we do more?"

I heard Lucas's forehead hit his desk with a loud thump.

"Oh, my," Ms. Marlowe said. "You can do as many hours as you like." She gave me a long look. "You know, Nick, at first I wasn't sure what to make of your being in this class. But I think you really mean what you've been saying. What a pleasure to see such a motivated and caring young man."

"I am who I am, Ms. Marlowe," I said. "Thank you for noticing."

"Oh, brother," I heard someone say. I prayed it wasn't Jennifer.

After class, Michelle caught up with Lucas and me and asked if we wanted some leads on baby-sitting jobs. Jennifer was with her.

"Jennifer just moved here," Michelle explained, "so I figured she'd need some names. You guys could probably use some, too." She looked at Lucas and smiled. "So you want to meet after school? Out by the circle?"

"Sure," I said. "Great."

Lucas didn't say anything. He just kept looking at Michelle in this funny way, as if he'd never seen her before or something.

It was a little like that when we met up after school, too. I mean, those two had known each other forever, but all of a sudden they were acting kind of goofy around each other. I didn't get it. As for Jennifer, well, she didn't seem to have her heart into getting baby-sitting leads. She kept running her fingers through her hair and looking off into space. I tried to engage her in conversation.

"You like movies?" I asked, thinking maybe I'd work up the nerve to ask her to one. Then I remembered asking her out was against the rules.

"Sure I like movies," Jennifer said. "Who doesn't?"

Grasping at straws, I blurted out, "Did you ever see *Bambi*?"

"*Bambi*?"

"Yeah, the one about the deer."

"I know what it's about. It's only my favorite movie ever."

"Honest?"

"Sure. I cry buckets."

"Me, too," I lied. "When the mother gets killed and Bambi's left all alone—"

"I cry *two* buckets at that part," Jennifer said. She studied me for a minute, then said, "I've never known a boy who cried—or admitted it, anyway. You're really . . . different, Nick."

"I'm kind of, you know, *sensitive*."

"I see that."

I shrugged. "It's like I told Ms. Marlowe—"

"You are who you are."

"Right." I tried looking sensitive. Jennifer smiled.

Just then, Mitch and Augie came into sight. Thanks to some fast thinking and quick footwork on my part, I squeezed in next to Jennifer and got my head so close to hers my nose closed up from her perfume.

"Better make sure we don't have the same names," I said, moving our two lists together.

I looked up then and waved at Mitch. As far apart as we were, I could see his face turning red. I swear, it almost looked as if steam was going to start coming out of his ears.

Yes! The Nickster scores!

Chapter 3:

So I Picked the Baby Up and Stuck It Under My Arm

"Do I have a volunteer?"

It was the next baby-sitting class. Ms. Marlowe was asking for someone to come up and put a diaper on a doll. My arm was in the air so fast it should have had NASA written on the sleeve.

"Nick," Ms. Marlowe said, calling on me. She looked pleased. I think she was really starting to like me.

Lucas whispered, "What're you, crazy?"

"What is the big deal about putting a diaper on a doll?" I whispered back. "Come on, Lucas, get with the program."

Unfortunately for me, just as I reached the front of the room, the program changed.

"Ah, perfect timing," I heard Ms. Marlowe say. Some of the girls in the class started to giggle. I hate when girls do that.

There in the doorway stood a woman about Ms. Marlowe's age. She was pushing something in a stroller. I knew what it was. I also knew I was in trouble.

"Our first little helper has arrived," Ms. Marlowe said, crossing to the woman and the thing in the stroller. "We won't have to use the doll after all. Nick, you did say you've changed diapers before, didn't you?"

"Oh yeah," I said. Lie. Big lie.

"And you've held babies?"

"Sure. Lots." Another lie. Hey, listen, I was already in over my head. The truth was I'd never held a baby in my life. I tried to think of what that article had said, something about women being impressed with men who held babies as easily as they held footballs. So I picked the baby up and stuck it under my arm.

The whole class started laughing, even Lucas, the traitor.

That was nothing compared to the actual changing of the diaper, however. Forget my turning totally red when I uncovered the evidence that the baby was a boy. I mean, who needs to have a bunch of girls staring at *that*? The really tough part though was trying to figure out how to get the old diaper off and the new one on without breaking the baby. Ms. Marlowe kept saying, "Are you *sure* you've changed diapers before, Nick?" and I kept saying, "Uh-huh, uh-huh," and nodding my head and all the time thinking, What do I do? What do I do?

At one point, I made the mistake of looking to Lucas for help, as if he'd have any better idea of what to do than I did. I'm an only child, and Lucas is the youngest of three kids. What did either of us know? The thing is, Lucas wasn't even watching me, he was staring at the door. He had this kind of queasy expression on his face, like he'd just scarfed down two dogs with chili sauce and a double order of fries.

Jennifer's eyes were on the door, too, but she didn't look queasy. She was smiling. I turned to check it out. Mistake.

Mitch and Augie were standing there. Mitch was winking at Jennifer, and Augie was doing his duh laugh (the silent version) while he gawked at me with the diaper in my hands. He nudged Mitch. Mitch turned and stared right at me. He made this face like, "Aw, isn't that cute?" and that's when the kid decided to pee.

I felt it first. All over my new shirt. When I looked down, I couldn't believe my eyes. Have you ever seen a baby pee? It's like a natural wonder of the world or something. I mean, if this kid had been twins it would have been the golden arches, know what I mean?

Mitch and Augie were cracking up—until Ms. Marlowe spotted them and shooed them away. But she was laughing while she did it. Everybody was laughing.

Jennifer, Lucas, the baby's mother—even the baby was smiling. I was the only one who didn't get the joke. That's because I *was* the joke.

Still, changing diapers was nothing compared to trying to get a baby-sitting job. I don't know what it was with me and kids. It was like they were allergic to me or something. At one job interview, the kid screamed so hard when I tried to pick him up his mother told me to leave before he ruptured his vocal cords. Another time, this five year old said I wore dorky sneakers and he'd never listen to anybody who wore dorky sneakers. I wear red high-tops. Is that dorky? Don't answer.

Anyway, I won't bore you with the rest of my efforts. Let's just say Lucas had already finished five out of his thirty baby-sitting hours while I was still ringing doorbells. Then my mom came to the rescue.

I was hanging out in a lounge chair on our patio, trying to get some homework done, while my mom messed around in her garden. She likes taking plants out of pots and sticking them in the ground and digging plants out of the ground and putting them into pots. Personally, it's not my thing, but she says getting her hands dirty helps her clear her head after a hard day at work.

Pooch had been lying on my left foot for so long it had fallen asleep. Every once in a while he'd raise his head to consider attacking a passing butterfly, twitch his tail for a few seconds, yawn, and settle his head back on my ankle. Pooch is one lazy cat.

"Oh, Nick," my mother said all of a sudden. "I forgot to tell you. I bumped into Sandy Coburn yesterday. You remember Sandy, don't you? Her ex-husband used to work for your father."

"Oh, her ex-husband is an ex-employee of my ex-father?" I said. I'm not usually sarcastic. Something about my father brings it out in me.

"Nick," my mother said in that let's-not-blame-your-father-for-the-divorce tone of voice she gets. I don't know why she still thinks she has to keep the peace all the time.

"Sorry, Mom."

"Anyway," she went on, shaking a couple of worms out of a clod of earth, "Sandy is having a hard time getting someone to stay with her son after school. It's a couple of hours every afternoon. Wouldn't that fulfill your class requirement?"

"I guess," I said, although I didn't love the idea of giving up every afternoon to play baby-sitter. I reminded myself that Jennifer was worth it.

"How old is this kid?" I asked.

"Seven. Almost eight, I think." She handed me a potted plant and asked if I would hang it from one of the hooks on the back wall of the house. She already had a ladder in place.

Now, there's something I have to tell you here that

I'm not exactly proud of. I mean, I'm not exactly ashamed of it, either, but if it wasn't important to my story I probably would skip bringing it up altogether. See, I have this thing about heights. I'm not scared exactly, more like terrified. I was kind of hoping all my pumping iron over the summer would make me a little tougher about heights, but what can I tell you? Just the thought of going up a ladder still turned my knees weak and my stomach to jelly.

My mom had twisted her ankle the day before. Otherwise, she probably wouldn't even have thought to ask me. I lifted Pooch off me (he let me know he wasn't happy about it), shook my foot out until some life started coming back to it, grabbed the geranium, and headed for the ladder.

Halfway up, I thought I was going to puke.

I guess it was pretty obvious. "Nick!" my mother called out. She ran to the ladder and took the plant out of my hands.

"I'm sorry," she said, keeping the ladder steady as I inched my way down. "I forgot you were afraid of heights."

Hey, I can admit this to *you*, but my mom is another story. "I'm not afraid," I insisted. "I just have this . . . thing."

"Whatever," Mom said. *Whatever* is what she always says when she's decided she's right and I won't admit it. "I'll take care of it myself when my ankle's better." She glanced at her watch. "Why don't you jump on your bike and go over to Sandy's? I told her you'd drop by when she got home from work."

I hadn't seen Mrs. Coburn in a long time. Our town is really small, like Lucas says, but the Coburns lived in the next town over. Which is all of maybe ten minutes by bike. Still, the kids there go to a different school, hang out at a different pizza place, rent their movies at a different video store. The only time we see each other is when our school, Calvin Coolidge, plays their school, Ralph Waldo Emerson.

Anyway, none of this has anything to do with Mrs. Coburn, but it does explain how I'd never seen Kelly before. But that's getting ahead of my story.

Mrs. Coburn was really happy to see me. She had lemonade waiting, and she offered me a dollar an hour more than any other baby-sitting job I'd tried for. I figured there had to be a hitch.

There was.

"Ben's an active child," Mrs. Coburn explained as she emptied a bag of expensive store-bought cookies onto a plate and shoved them in front of me. "He has a wonderful imagination. And he's very smart. Have some cookies."

I began wondering why she had had a hard time finding a baby-sitter for such an active, wonderful, smart kid. I was also wondering why I wasn't meeting him. But I kept my wondering to myself. After all, beggars can't be choosers, and at this point I needed this job as much as Mrs. Coburn needed me. If she'd known the truth, she could have saved on cookies and lemonade.

"Um, where is Ben exactly?" I asked.

"Out back," she said. "Oh, the two of you are going to get along so well, Nick. I can just feel it in my bones. Would you like another glass of lemonade?"

"I think I'd like to meet Ben," I told her.

She smiled. It was one of those mysterious smiles, like the one in that painting of Mona Lisa. "He's out back," she said again.

The backyard wasn't big. It had trees, clothes on a line, some lawn chairs, and no Ben. I looked around for about five minutes.

"Ben," I called. "Yo, Ben."

Nothing.

Nothing but this girl, that is. She wasn't in the yard exactly. She was in the yard next door, hanging over the fence, and saying, "Hi."

"Hi," I said back. I guessed that she was about my age. She had long brown hair and these big eyes and the kind of healthy-looking face my mother calls well scrubbed. I always thought that was a weird thing to call a face. A potato maybe, but not a face. "What are you doing there?" I asked.

She laughed. "Watching you," she said. "What are you doing *there*?"

"Baby-sitting. Can't you tell?"

"For Ben?"

I nodded.

"Well, if you're baby-sitting for him, where is he?"

"Beats me. His mother said he was out here. He does exist, doesn't he?"

That really got her laughing. "Oh, he exists all right, believe me. I don't think I've seen you before. Do you go to Emerson?"

"Coolidge," I said. "Ninth grade."

"Me, too. I'm Kelly."

"I'm Nick."

"Hi, Nick."

"Hi, Kelly."

We both laughed. I noticed Kelly's well-scrubbed face getting kind of red. "Where have you looked for Ben?" she asked.

"Everywhere," I told her. "It isn't that big a yard."

"Have you looked up?"

"Up?"

"Look up. Ben loves to climb."

I was about to follow Kelly's advice when something landed and exploded on my head. Water dripped down my face. Kelly laughed.

"Gotcha, turkey!" a voice called out.

Wiping my eyes, I looked up. Ben, the climber of trees and thrower of water balloons, looked down at me from high up in the branches, an evil grin plastered on his face.

"Nick, meet Ben," Kelly said.

"Turkey!" Ben shouted. I wondered if all the lemonade and cookies in the world was worth it. For a second or two there, I even wondered if Jennifer was worth it.

But then I thought about winning the bet and beating Mitch.

"Ben Coburn!" I shouted. "I'm going to get you for that!"

Chapter 4:

My Worst Nightmare

Let me put it this way: Ben was my worst nightmare.

Well, maybe not my *worst* nightmare. I started having these dreams about wearing a tutu and doing this little dance in the middle of the gym. In front of every kid in the school. All of whom were laughing. Mitch hardest of all.

And then I had this one dream where my dad was there, too. He had his arm draped around Mitch's shoulders, and the two of them were pointing at me and carrying on like a couple of hyenas.

But those were only dreams. Ben was real.

Every time I went to his house he had a surprise planned. And they weren't the kinds of surprises Lucas's kid, Jeremy, had. Jeremy surprised Lucas with a piece of cake his mom had made the night before or a softball for the two of them to toss around. Not Ben. He'd hide. Sometimes he'd hide out back with a water balloon. Sometimes he'd be in his bedroom armed with a squirt gun. Between sitting for Ben and changing diapers in class, I was beginning to think I should have myself coated in Teflon. Anyway, it was true what Kelly had said about Ben. He loved to climb. He was all over those backyard trees of his. I called him Little Monkey. He called me Big Turkey. Kind of chokes you up, doesn't it?

Whenever I suggested we do something together, he'd shrug and say, "Who wants to do *that*? It's dumb."

After a few days, I gave up. I'd let him do anything he wanted while I did my homework. That was all right for a while. Then he started saying stuff like, "How come we never *do* anything? I'm going to tell my mom you don't do anything with me and she shouldn't pay you so much."

"Believe me, Ben," I'd say, "there's no way your mom could pay me too much for this job."

Then he'd throw something at me, and I'd yell at him, and he'd yell at me. And that was how it went. Every afternoon.

Naturally, I didn't tell anyone what was going on. Except Pooch. And Lucas. I was beginning to wonder if it was all worth it. Jennifer hardly seemed to notice I was alive, let alone that I was the most sensitive guy on the face of the earth.

The only class we had together was baby-sitting and child care, so that was where I had my best shot at getting her attention. But, hey, the class itself hardly got her attention. When she wasn't brushing her hair, she was writing in this book with flowers all over the cover. I tried to sneak a peek at what she was writing in there, but she always had her arm over it so you couldn't see. I began wondering why she was taking the class in the first place. Ms. Marlowe was always having to remind her to put down her brush or her book and participate. Even Michelle seemed to be getting fed up with her.

But I couldn't give up. Too much was at stake. Like, for instance, total humiliation. I was sure I could still impress Jennifer with my sensitive ways. Don't forget, this was a girl whose favorite movie was *Bambi*.

One day in class I started going on and on about my great relationship with Ben. "Oh yeah, I call Ben Little Monkey and he, well, he has a special name for me, too." I glanced at the magazine lying open on my lap. "Uh, um, see, I think Ben is responding to me as a positive male role model. That's it. He sees me as . . . " and now I read directly from the article, "'as the kind of guy who's tough when he needs to be, but knows how to be as gentle as a newborn lamb.'"

I heard giggles. Looking up, I saw Ms. Marlowe staring at me with her mouth hanging open. Lucas's mouth was hanging open, too. I looked at Jennifer. Her mouth wasn't open, but her brush was stuck in her hair.

"You're an interesting young man," I heard Ms. Marlowe say.

"Thank you," I said. "I think." I looked down at the top of my desk and wished I could sink into a pool of quicksand and Lucas wouldn't save me.

"Tell me," Ms. Marlowe went on bravely, "are there any activities the two of you enjoy doing together?"

Oh, sure, I thought: swapping insults, dodging flying objects, threatening bodily harm. But instead of these, I came out with: "Basketball."

This was partly true. The part that was true was that I liked basketball. To put it mildly, Ben didn't. I found this out the first time I took him to practice with me, and he hid all the towels while everybody was in the showers. He threatened not to tell us where they were unless I promised never to make him come with me to practice again.

Believe me, that's one promise I wished I could have made. But junior varsity practice started early in the year. We met twice a week after school, so I didn't have any choice but to drag Ben along with me. That meant being late because I had to ride my bike over to his school, pick him up, ride him back to my school, and change.

None of this went down too well with the coach, a guy in his thirties named Mr. Rose. We don't call him that; we call him Coach. He lives on my street, but even when I see him around the neighborhood I call him Coach. I was lucky he did live on my street. Since he'd known me my whole life, he gave me a break on this Ben thing. I mean, I could've been dropped from the team for being late, but Coach Rose was willing to overlook it.

Still, even Coach had his limits.

The very afternoon I'd told my class how much the little monkey and I liked basketball, Ben lay down in the middle of the court and refused to move. I hate to admit it, but I was beginning to admire anybody who'd go to such extremes to get his point across.

"I hate basketball," Ben said through gritted teeth when I asked what he was doing there.

"Well, that's too bad," I told him. "Now wait where I told you to."

"I don't have to do what you tell me," he shot back. "I don't know why I have to be here at all."

"I told you why. A couple of afternoons a week—"

Suddenly Mitch's face was in mine. "Could you get your little friend off the court, Nicky?" he sneered. "Or didn't they teach you how to handle stuff like this in baby class?"

"Watch it, Mitch," I said.

"Ooh, is that a threat, Kramer?"

"Yes, it is, *Buckley*."

"What're you going to do? Throw a diaper at me?"

Just then, I felt the coach's hand on my shoulder. "Chill, you two," he said. Then he looked down at Ben.

There was a long moment while Coach let out a sigh that whistled through his teeth.

"Nick, we have here what I'd call a situation."

"Yes sir."

"Are you equipped to do something about this situation?"

"Yes sir," I repeated, my mind scrambling to come up with a solution. The first step was clear: get Ben off the court.

"With me, Monkey," I said in a tone of voice even he knew meant business. *"Now."* I didn't wait for him to cooperate. Grabbing him by the collar, I dragged him across the floor and out of the gym.

By the time we got out in the hall, I was seeing red. I pinned Ben against the wall and said, "If you ever pull a stunt like that again—" But I didn't get any further. Following the sudden shift of Ben's eyes, I saw none other than Jennifer Edwards coming down the hall—and right in my direction. My heart skipped a beat. My hands got sweaty. I looked back at Ben and thought: a perfect chance to show my stuff!

Releasing Ben, I roughed up his hair affectionately, bent down as if he'd just asked me a question, and said in a gentle, nurturing voice, "What's that you asked, Ben?"

He looked at me as if I'd gone nuts. "I didn't ask anything," he said.

I laughed good-naturedly. "Good question, Ben," I

said in a loud voice to make sure Jennifer would hear. "You're such a smart kid. That's one of the many reasons I enjoy taking care of you every afternoon."

"Huh?" Ben said.

"Oh, Jennifer, hi," I said, acting surprised as Jennifer walked by.

Ben looked at me and said, "What's with you all of a sudden?"

Jennifer glanced at her watch. "Hi," she said. She kept moving, so I grabbed Ben by the shoulders and moved him alongside her.

"There's someone I want you to meet," I told Jennifer.

"Another time," Jennifer said.

"This is Ben. You know, *Ben*."

"That's nice. I have a doctor's appointment, Nick."

Wow. Another golden opportunity. "Are you okay, Jennifer?" I asked, contorting my face into the most sensitive expression I could muster. "Do you need a friend to go with you? Do you want to talk about it?"

Jennifer stopped walking and looked at me the way she sometimes does in baby-sitting class. Ben was looking at me, too. All of a sudden he got this gleam in his eye. I didn't like the looks of it.

"I'm fine, really," Jennifer said. "It's just a check-up."

"Oh," I said, "that's a relief. Anyway, the little monkey here was just asking me about some of the fine points of the game. He *begged* me to bring him with me to practice. So where were we, Ben?"

"Gee, I think you were telling me about dribbling, Rick."

"Nick," I reminded him, under my breath. What was that about?

Ben slapped his forehead with the palm of his hand. "Right, it's *Nick*," he said. And then he started pouring out this story so fast and so thick I couldn't stop it—and Jennifer couldn't move. "I can never remember his name," Ben went on. "See, this is the first time he's let me out of the cellar since he's been sitting for me. Oh, the cellar has heat and everything. There's even a lightbulb down there. And sometimes, Jack—I mean, Rick—gives me an old comic book to read and maybe even a couple of crackers for a snack. And there's a faucet where I can get water, even if it is a little rusty. See this?"

He showed Jennifer a scratch on the back of his hand.

"I had to fight off a rat for one of my crackers a couple of days ago."

Jennifer gasped. "Nick Kramer!" she said, spitting out my name like it was poison or something. "Wait until I tell Ms. Marlowe."

"Jennifer, stop!" I called out as she raced toward the door. "He's kidding, honest. He's a great kidder."

She was gone. Behind my back, Ben was laughing hysterically. The only thing that saved his rotten little seven-year-old life at that moment was the appearance of Coach Rose.

"Kramer!" he shouted.

It took me a few seconds before I could move. I couldn't believe what a mess everything was. Jennifer thought I was a monster, Coach thought I couldn't handle a bratty kid, the bratty kid thought he could walk all over me, and Mitch . . . well, I didn't know what Mitch thought. Until I walked back into the gym, that is.

"Yo, Nickster," he called out, aiming a basketball right at my gut, "looks like you play mommy about as good as you play ball!"

Chapter 5:

Pooch, What Am I Doing Wrong?

The next morning, I opened my eyes to find Pooch staring into them. If you've never woken up to discover a cat's face in yours, it can be a little scary. I was used to it. Pooch often gets his day started by sitting on my chest and staring at me until my eyes open. He always has this serious expression on his face, which makes me want to ask him serious questions.

This particular morning, I had lots of them. "Pooch, what am I doing wrong? How can I get Jennifer to like me, or at least ask me to the Vice-Versa Dance? Will I ever have a girlfriend? What's the matter with me anyhow?"

Pooch sneezed in my face. He's a good listener, but he doesn't give the best advice.

Lucas was about as helpful. Walking to school, he kept playing his harmonica while I poured out my soul, then stopped long enough to inform me that he liked Michelle's hats. Michelle does wear these funky hats, it's true, but I never thought that was something Lucas would notice or care about. Besides, didn't he know I wanted to talk about *me*?

By the time I picked Ben up from his school and walked him home, I was totally depressed. Letting him run ahead of me, I was so out of it I walked right into this girl and knocked her down. It turned out to be Kelly.

"Gee, I'm sorry," I said, helping her up. She looked mad at first, but then she got all flustered and smiled.

"It's you," she said, brushing herself off and collecting all the books and papers that had fallen out of her backpack.

"Are you hurt?" I asked.

"I'm okay. Just surprised. Um, you want an apple? I have an extra from lunch."

I couldn't figure out why she was being so nice. The way I'd crashed into her, she could've broken her arm or something. But considering how many people had been angry at me lately, I was glad she was being nice. Really glad.

She was holding an apple out to me. "So?" she said.

I looked at Ben's house. He was in there—*waiting*.

"Sure," I said.

We sat down on Ben's front steps, and I bit into the apple. I looked at Kelly out of the corner of my eyes. She was nice. Pretty, too. Not pretty like Jennifer, a simpler kind of pretty. Jennifer was like one of those perfect living rooms people have where you can tell they've spent lots of money but nobody's allowed to sit in it. Kelly was more like a den with comfortable furniture where you can hang out and watch TV.

Does that make sense?

"A penny for your thoughts," Kelly said.

I almost choked on the apple. No way was I going to tell her what I'd just been thinking. Luckily, Kelly went on talking.

"My mom says that all the time. She thinks I'm too quiet. She just doesn't understand that I'm different from her and Liz."

"Who's Liz?" I asked.

"My sister. She's in college now, premed. She's going to be a surgeon."

"Neat," I brilliantly interjected.

"I don't know what I want to be yet," Kelly went on. "I like science, but I don't want to be a doctor like Liz. Blood is definitely not my thing. What about you?"

"Is blood my thing? But of course," I said, trying on a Transylvanian accent for size. It was a loose fit. "I am . . . Count Dracula!"

I made a vampire face, which cracked Kelly up. "You have a piece of apple stuck to one of your fangs," she said, laughing. "Anyway, I didn't mean that. I meant do you know what you want to be?"

I shrugged. "All that seems so far away," I said. "I'm just trying to get through ninth grade. One thing is for sure. I do *not* want to be a baby-sitter."

This made Kelly laugh some more. I tried to keep track of all the funny things I was saying. Maybe they would work on Jennifer.

Kelly shook her head. "It's not going so good with Ben, huh?"

"I think the word is bad. No, terrible. No, wait, that's not it. Horrendoscious. Is that a word?"

"It sounds right," Kelly said. "Mrs. Coburn hasn't found a sitter yet who stays longer than a couple of weeks."

"Did you ever sit for Ben?" I asked.

Kelly nodded. "He's okay with me. I guess because we've known each other so long. He's tough, but he's a good kid really."

"So why don't *you* sit for him every afternoon?"

"I can't. I have a heavy workload this year. I'm under strict orders from my parents: afternoons are for homework. Anyway, if I sat for Ben you'd be out of a job, right? It's kind of unusual, isn't it?"

"What?" I asked.

"A boy baby-sitter."

"Oh, that." I told her about the class and the thirty hours of baby-sitting, but I didn't say anything about the bet with Mitch.

"I think it's really cool that you and your friend are taking that class," she said when I'd finished.

"You do?"

"Yeah. More guys should do stuff like that."

Wow. Somebody who liked sensitive guys, at last.

She didn't stay impressed long, though. When I told her what happened at basketball practice, she said she didn't think Ben's little show in front of Jennifer was any worse than mine.

"What are you talking about?" I asked. "Ben made a total fool of me."

"Yeah, but you made a fool of Ben first, pretending that you liked him and that you thought he was so smart and everything. And all to show off in front of this girl, what's her name again? Jennifer?" I nodded. "Why can't you just be yourself?"

I had to laugh at that one. "I've been myself for fourteen years," I said. "And the closest I've come to getting a girl to notice me was when my Aunt Louise said I had a smile like some actor on TV. So I watched his show and tried being him for three weeks. That didn't work, either."

Kelly shook her head. "What is it with guys?" she asked. "Why do you always have to try to be something you're not? What if you just *talked* to Jennifer? You could *tell* her you like her."

"Talk?" I said, my voice cracking. "I can't talk to girls."

"You're talking to me, aren't you?"

I was surprised. I *was* talking to Kelly, who was, in fact, a girl. "You're different," I said.

Kelly's smile disappeared right off her face. "I should get going," she said. "Homework."

"Okay. Well, thanks for the apple. It was nice bumping into you."

Kelly picked up her backpack.

"Get it?" I said. "It was nice *bumping* into you."

She looked at me blankly. "Oh, right," she said.

I watched her cross the yard to her house next door and wondered what had happened to her sense of humor. Anyway, her advice was good.

I thought a lot about what she had said. *Talk* to Jennifer. It sounded great in theory, but even if I could get up the nerve, Jennifer was always with other people. To make matters worse, "other people" usually included Mitch.

The next day, Lucas and I were turning the corner to the cafeteria when we spotted Jennifer and Lindsay walking ahead of us with Mitch and Augie. They were all laughing a lot. I noticed that Mitch and Jennifer were laughing hardest of all.

"I give up," I said to Lucas. "As in, I quit!"

"Is this the new Nick Kramer I hear?" Lucas said.

"Do me a favor, Lucas. Don't bust my chops. And, by the way, where'd you get that hat?" Lucas was wearing this truly weird hat.

"Michelle gave it to me in English," he said. "What, you don't like it?"

I could see he was ready to get seriously offended, so I lied. "It's great. I just wondered where you got it, is all."

"Oh."

Jennifer's laughter rang out ahead as she poked Mitch's arm playfully. I groaned.

Lucas said, "Listen, Nick, you've still got a few weeks until the Vice-Versa Dance. By some miracle, Jennifer hasn't asked Mitch yet."

"Yeah," I said, "and it'll take an even greater miracle for her to ask me. Now I know what girls go through. This is the *pits*, Lucas."

"Stop feeling sorry for yourself. Look, if you want to win this bet with Mitch, you've got to make it happen. Create the opportunity."

Before I could ask what he meant, a girl's voice said, "Nice hat."

It was Michelle, wearing a long skirt that went almost to the floor. Lucas bowed dramatically, waving his hat around like he was in a play by Shakespeare. Michelle curtsied. So there they were: the king and queen of funk. And there I was: the court jester.

"Want to sit with us at lunch?" Michelle asked me as we entered the cafeteria. I shot Lucas a look. Wasn't *he* supposed to be asking *her* to sit with *us*?

As it turned out, the three of us sat at the same table as Jennifer, Lindsay, Mitch, and Augie. Which would have been great if I'd been able to sit anywhere near Jennifer, but I was at one end and she was at the other. The whole time I kept thinking about Kelly's advice and Lucas's.

Talk to Jennifer. Make it happen. Create the opportunity.

But how?

"Why don't we get a pizza and rent a movie?" I heard Lindsay saying. I noticed that Lindsay was getting very buddy-buddy with Jennifer. She'd even started wearing her hair the same way, and she had the same kind of big dangly earrings. I looked at Lucas and Michelle with their hats, and Lindsay and Jennifer with their hair and earrings, and began wondering if there was some sort of invasion of the body snatchers thing going on at Calvin Coolidge High.

"Sounds good," Jennifer said. She turned to Mitch and practically purred, "Don't you think?"

Mitch looked at me with this smug look plastered all over his face like a billboard ad. "Sure," he said. Then he quickly turned back to Jennifer and said, "But it's not a date thing, right?"

Jennifer's expression turned sour. "What?"

"Am I right?" Mitch asked.

Lindsay said, "That's so weird, Mitch."

"I'm just asking a question," Mitch said, starting to get a little red. It was nice to see him squirm. I was enjoying it.

"Yeah, he was just axing a question," Augie echoed. Augie always says "ax" for "ask."

Jennifer kept looking at Mitch with the same sour expression. I was enjoying that, too.

"Oh, wait," she said all of a sudden. "I can't believe it. I have to baby-sit tonight."

"No! That's so unfair," Lindsay said as if Jennifer had just announced she'd been grounded for the rest of her life.

Mitch said, "Maybe you can work something out, Jen."

Jen. I caught that.

Jennifer smiled sweetly. "Maybe," she said.

The bell rang and we all scrambled to clear our trays. I couldn't believe my luck. Jennifer had just handed me my opportunity. As I walked to baby-sitting class, my mind was ticking away on the perfect plan to make it happen.

Luckily, we spent the class out in the playground with a bunch of three year olds. This made it easy to move around. I kept my eye on Jennifer, who was pushing a little boy on a swing and filing her nails at the same time.

When Ms. Marlowe got involved in breaking up a fight in the sandbox, I moved in on Jennifer. "Hi, there," I said.

She glared at me. "I haven't told Ms. Marlowe about that boy you keep locked in the cellar yet," she said. "But I will."

"Oh, come on, Jen," I said, trying the familiar approach, "you know he was kidding. Do you seriously think I'd lock Ben in the cellar? What kind of guy do you think I am?"

"Strange," she said. And then she added, "But kind of sweet."

"Like sauerkraut with chocolate sauce." I smiled. She didn't.

I decided to take the conversation in a new direction. "Look," I said, "I *don't* lock Ben in the cellar, okay? But sometimes I don't know *what* to do with him. I watch you with kids and you're such a natural."

"Me?" She almost pushed the boy off the swing.

Taking a deep breath, I plunged into the next step of my plan. "I'll bet you get along great with that girl you sit for, what's her name?"

"Alyssa?"

"Yeah, Alyssa. The way you talk about her in class . . ." The truth was I don't think Jennifer had ever said anything about her in class. "Well, I could really use some advice."

Jennifer gave me a doubting look. "Mr. Mom wants my advice about kids?"

"Yeah." Another deep breath. "Say, I have a great idea. What if I come over to your house tonight and—"

"No, Nick, that isn't a great idea," Jennifer said, cutting me off. Then her face brightened up. "Wait. I have to sit tonight, remember? Why don't you come over to Alyssa's house? I can give you some baby-sitting tips and we can, like, hang out, y'know?"

This was going better than I'd imagined.

"Great!" I said.

"Alyssa lives on Sycamore. Her last name is Michaels."

"Oh, *that* Alyssa," I said. "Her father was my Cub Scout leader." I grinned. "Small town. Everybody knows everybody."

"Good," Jennifer said. "Then they won't mind if you're there."

"No. At least, I don't think so."

"Good," she said again, more to herself than to me. Then to me she said, "This will be fun, Nick. It'll be a chance for us to get to know each other better." She smiled and I thought my knees were going to give out. It was the same smile she'd been smiling at Mitch an hour before. Only this time it was for me.

Me. Nick Kramer. Mr. Mom.

Chapter 6:

All That Mattered Was Jennifer— and My Hair

A strange thing happened at Ben's that afternoon. We actually *did* something together. Ben had this dinosaur kit that had just come in the mail, and as soon as I got there, he asked me to do it with him.

"Who, me?" I asked.

"No, turkey, your brother."

"I don't have a brother," I told him.

"So that's two of us," he said. "Are you going to help me or what?"

"Sure." I stood back while he opened the box, positive that something was going to jump out at me.

But nothing did. We spent the next hour—with time out to make popcorn—putting this dinosaur together. And nothing bad happened. Ben didn't run out of the room and return with a water balloon. He didn't call me any more names. Mostly, he whistled.

At one point, he said, "My dad sent this kit. And

you're helping me put it together." That's all. Then he started whistling again. I wondered what he was talking about, but I didn't ask. Whatever was making him happy, I didn't want to mess with it.

Of course, I was in a good mood, too. I was going to spend the evening with Jennifer. I kept thinking about how she'd said we'd hang out together. I tried to imagine what that would be like. I guess I was daydreaming when the doorbell rang. I heard Kelly ask if I was there and Ben answer, "Sort of."

"Kelly!" I called out as she came into the living room.

Her whole face lit up. "Hi, Nick," she said.

"Guess what. Your advice worked," I told her.

"What advice?"

"About girls. I talked to Jennifer and I'm seeing her tonight. Isn't that great?"

"Great," Kelly said, but her smile was gone. I was beginning to notice that Kelly's smile had a habit of disappearing without warning. Lucas says girls are moody. At least, he used to say that.

Kelly picked up a magazine from the coffee table and flipped through its pages without really looking at them. She said, "That's what you wanted, right?"

"Right!"

"So congratulations, I guess." Kelly put down the magazine and picked up the dinosaur. "Did you do this?" she asked Ben.

Ben said, "Yeah, Nick and I did it. Isn't it cool? Hey, Nick, we still have some pieces to—"

Just then I noticed the time. "Oh no!" I cried. "I've only got three hours! I've got to go home and get ready. Kelly, could you do me a favor?"

"I guess so," she said. "What?"

"Would you mind staying with Ben till his mom gets home?" I jumped up before Kelly could answer. "Thanks. You're a real friend. If there's anything I can ever do for you . . . "

And I was out of there.

Okay, so I acted like a jerk. It was bad enough I didn't help Ben finish the dinosaur, but to pull a number like that on Kelly . . . well, what can I tell you? I wasn't thinking clearly, okay? All that mattered was Jennifer—and my hair.

I guess I should explain about my hair. I told you I got this cool haircut when school started, and that's true. But my hair kind of has a mind of its own. After a while, these things called cowlicks take over. Since I was due for a haircut, the cowlicks ruled. That's why I decided to try mousse. I'd never used it before, but I figured it was bound to keep my hair where I wanted it to go.

By the time my mom came into my room, I had practically used the whole can of mousse, and my hair still had a mind of its own. As for my room, well, let's just say that every piece of clothing I owned was on my bed, on the floor, or on me.

"Knock, knock," my mom said, entering the room without knocking. I hate when she does that. She took a look around and shook her head. "Was World War III just fought in here or . . ." She smiled when she saw me.

Now, a cool thing about my mom is that she doesn't get mad about stuff like messy rooms. But an uncool thing is the way she gets when she thinks I look cute.

"Why, Nick Kramer," she said as if I were a baby chick she couldn't wait to pick up and nuzzle, "do you have a *date*?"

It didn't help that she said "date" as if it was the last word in the world she'd think to use in the same sentence with "Nick Kramer."

Then, to add insult to injury, she asked, "What did you do to your hair?"

"It's mousse, Mom, okay? And do you have to say 'do you have a date' like that?"

"Like what?" she asked, looking hurt.

"Like it's cute. Anyway, it's not a date . . . exactly."

I changed my shirt one last time. Red. To match my sneakers.

"Do you like this shirt?" I asked my mother.

She looked at me, her eyes getting all soft and wet

like sunny-side-up eggs. "You look very handsome," she said, wiping, I swear, a tear from her eye.

"Mom, I'm going out for a couple of hours. I'm not going off to college."

She laughed. "I know. It's just that you're growing up."

Why does she always say this like it's news or something?

On my way out of the house, it occurred to me I should take something to Jennifer. Flowers would be good. Flowers are what Mitch would take. But at seven o'clock there was nowhere open I could get flowers. Candy would also be good, I thought. My mom had gone grocery shopping that day. I scoped out the unpacked bags on the kitchen table to see what I could come up with.

"Doughnuts," Jennifer said twenty minutes later as I handed her the long rectangular box. "Gosh, I don't know what to say." Her eyes strayed to the top of my head. "What did you do to your hair?" she asked.

Just then, Alyssa came running to the door. "Doughnuts!" she shouted. "Can I have—"

Jennifer slammed the box into the poor kid's rib cage. "Gee, thanks," Alyssa said, running off.

Stepping into the house, I said, "Is that okay?"

Jennifer shrugged. "Is what okay?" she asked. I noticed that she was pretty dressed up for baby-sitting. Then I reminded myself that I'd gotten all duded up, too. Maybe my fantasies were running away with me, but I began thinking that Jennifer had put as much time into getting ready for this date-that-wasn't-a-date as I did.

I saw Alyssa biting into her second doughnut. "Has Alyssa eaten dinner?" I asked. "I wouldn't want her to get sick or anything."

"Don't worry about it," Jennifer said, leading me into the living room, where I took the box of dough-nuts out of Alyssa's hands. "Save some for later," I whispered.

"I can give her anything I want," Jennifer went on. "Her parents trust me."

Just the cue I was waiting for. Alyssa hit the remote control and started watching the news. Since she was only a little kid, I wasn't sure this was a great idea, but I didn't say anything about it. Instead, I threw the old conversational ball back to Jennifer.

"Right," I said, "see, that's what I've got to learn. How do you get their trust?"

"Trust," Jennifer repeated. "Um, let's see . . ."

Before she got any farther, the phone rang. Alyssa ran to get it, but Jennifer was there first and practically drew blood getting it out of the poor kid's hands. I felt so bad for Alyssa I handed her another doughnut.

"Hello. Oh, hi, Mom." I don't know what was said next on the other end, but from the way Jennifer's face caved in I knew it had to be serious.

"What? Oh, no! When? Is he going to be all right?" She began dabbing her perfectly polished fingernails at her perfectly made-up eyes.

The next thing I knew she was crying. Alyssa stopped watching the news to stare at Jennifer, although I noticed she didn't stop eating her doughnut.

"Yes, all right," Jennifer said into the phone. "I will, Mom. Bye."

Slowly, she put down the telephone. She was making these little choking noises in her throat. "Jennifer? Is anything wrong?" I asked.

"It's my dad," she said, and then she started crying so hard her eyeliner began running down her cheeks.

Alyssa and I looked at each other. I don't know what was on the kid's mind, but I knew what was on mine. I just wasn't sure how to say it. "Is your dad, you know . . ."

Jennifer looked at me. I shoved my facial muscles all over the place, giving them a real workout, as if that somehow was supposed to convey the word *dead*.

"What? Oh, no. No," Jennifer said to my great relief. "But it's bad, Nick. I have to go." She reached for her purse, which was lying on the sofa, then stopped herself. "But I can't go."

She looked at Alyssa, who was chewing in slow motion.

"Oh, what am I going to do?" Jennifer cried.

I wanted to put my arms around her, but I was afraid she'd take it the wrong way. Or the right way. But anyway, it just didn't feel like the thing to do. Instead, I said, "Would you like me to stay with Alyssa?"

This cheered Jennifer right up. "Oh, would you, Nick?"

I looked over at Alyssa, who had this huge grin on her face. She probably figured I'd let her polish off the box of doughnuts the first five minutes Jennifer was out of there.

"Sure," I said.

Jennifer came over and squeezed my hand. I think my heart stopped for a maybe a second or two there. "Thank you, Nick," she said, looking me right in the eyes. "You're just about the nicest guy I know."

She gave my hand an extra little squeeze, grabbed her purse, and headed for the door.

"Oh, Alyssa's bedtime is eight-thirty. Her parents should be home by ten." A buzzer sounded somewhere. "That's her dinner. Bye."

"Bye," I said to the slamming door.

I looked at Alyssa and she looked at me. This evening was not turning out the way either of us had planned. But then, things weren't turning out so great for Jennifer, either.

"Buzzer," Alyssa said.

"What?"

"Maybe you should turn off the buzzer."

"Right," I said, and headed for the kitchen, where Alyssa's dinner was waiting. Standing in somebody else's kitchen, my hair moussed to the point of sculpture, Jennifer gone, and a kid in the other room eating an entire box of doughnuts I'd actually had the nerve to think was a suitable token of romance, I had this urge to pick up the phone and call Pooch.

"Pooch," I would say, picturing his serious little tabby face listening intently on the other end, "what am I doing here?"

I returned to reality before giving Pooch a chance to sneeze.

Chapter 7:
Florida

Reality for Alyssa meant a dinner that looked like a failed science experiment.

"My mom does stuff with leftovers," she explained, her enthusiasm for doughnuts taking on new meaning.

"Do you think your parents would be real upset if we went out for pizza?" I asked. "Antonio's is two blocks from here—"

"I know," Alyssa interrupted, her eyes lighting up and her feet heading for the door. "All my sitters take me there."

I laughed. "They do, huh?"

Alyssa nodded. "Except for Jennifer," she said. "She says pizza is fattening."

"Do you like Jennifer?" I asked, as we moved outside. It was a perfect night to be out for a walk. I

wouldn't have minded being with someone closer to
my own age, but Alyssa wasn't bad company. For a kid.

"She's okay," Alyssa said. "*You* like her, I can tell."

I think I blushed. I was going to have to get used
to the fact that the new Nick Kramer was as easily
embarrassed as the old one.

By the time we got to Antonio's, we weren't talking about Jennifer anymore. I found out that Alyssa
was six and in first grade. I also found out that we had
a lot of things in common: we both loved the Oz
books, the New York Knicks, and pizza with pepperoni.

"I guess we'd better get a large," I said as the
familiar blast of air-conditioning welcomed us to
Antonio's.

"With extra pepperoni," Alyssa said.

Right away, I caught a glimpse of Mitch sitting at a
corner table with Augie and Lindsay.

"Yo, Nickster!" Mitch called as I steered Alyssa in
their direction.

I noticed two unopened pizza boxes sitting on
the table. "Hi, Mitch," I said. "You guys sure must be
hungry."

Ignoring me, Mitch shoved his face into Alyssa's.
"And who is this pretty young lady?" he asked. Alyssa
disappointed me by being charmed.

"This is Alyssa," I told him.

"Alyssa. Nice name." He offered her some potato

chips. What a smooth operator, I thought, even with the grade-school crowd. "So, Nicky," he said, "you expanding your baby-sitting empire?"

Augie did his duh laugh. Lindsay giggled. The perfect couple.

"Yeah, very funny," I said to Mitch. "As a matter of fact, I'm helping Jennifer out. Her dad's real sick or something."

"Is that so?" Mitch said, scrunching up his face like he cared.

"Listen, Mitch, I know you make fun of that class, but it just so happens Jennifer and I are pretty tight because of it."

Mitch's upper lip curled. "Yeah," he said, "right."

"So what're you guys doing here?" I asked.

Mitch said, "Just hanging out, Kramer. It's what some of us refer to as a social life."

I curled my own upper lip then, ready to put Mitch in his place, when all of a sudden Augie said, "It's not like a *date* thing."

Mitch jabbed Augie's right arm, while Lindsay got him from the left.

"What do you mean?" I started to ask, but at that moment Alyssa, reaching for some potato chips, knocked over a jumbo soda. It went all over the table and onto Lindsay, who jumped up, sending cascades of cola and crushed ice all over the floor. I grabbed some napkins to help clean up the mess, but Mitch yanked them out of my hands. "No problem, no problem," he said. "I'll clean that up. It's cool."

"But—"

"Don't worry about it."

"I could get a mop," I suggested.

"I'm sorry," Alyssa said in a small voice.

Mitch patted her gently on the shoulder. "Hey, accidents happen," he told her. "Don't sweat it, okay?" He grabbed one of the unopened pizza boxes and said, "Listen, you guys like pepperoni?"

Alyssa and I looked at each other. Did we like pepperoni?

"Take it," Mitch said.

"But I can't—"

"Listen, I don't want Alyssa to feel bad, okay? Take it. My treat."

Since when was Mitch such a nice guy? I shrugged. "If you don't want it," I said.

"Settled," Mitch retorted, shoving the box into my hands. "See you at school tomorrow, okay, Nickster? Bye, Alyssa."

"Bye," Alyssa said, smiling sweetly. As we turned to go, she whispered loudly, "He's nice."

I wanted to tell her the truth about guys like Mitch, but my eye was caught by something familiar on the table. "Isn't that Jennifer's purse?" I asked. I could swear I had seen Jennifer leave with one just like it.

Lindsay looked at it, then at me. "It's mine," she said simply.

"Oh," I said. Lindsay was turning into a major Jennifer clone. It was scary.

I spent the rest of the evening eating pizza and playing Chutes and Ladders with Alyssa. She beat me two out of three. Alyssa told me I was the best baby-sitter she ever had, which a few weeks earlier wouldn't have meant much, but after all I'd been through with Ben, it meant a lot, believe me.

When Alyssa's parents came home, they said, "Hi, Nick," as if they'd expected to find me there. They told me Jennifer had said I was coming over, but they were surprised to hear about her dad. "I guess it was lucky for her—and for us—that you were here," they said. "Everything go okay?"

"Great," I told them. "We had fun." And that was the truth.

Walking home, I kept thinking I should have been disappointed at how the evening turned out. But I wasn't really. I had a good time, was a few dollars richer, and at bedtime I got to read Alyssa chapter sixteen of *The Emerald City of Oz*, which only happens to be my favorite chapter of my favorite Oz book.

The next morning at school, I spotted Jennifer and Lindsay outside their homeroom. They were laughing, but as soon as Jennifer saw me coming, she stopped and started tugging at Lindsay's sleeve.

"Hi, Jennifer," I said.

"Oh, Nick, hi," she said, avoiding my eyes and picking at her nails. I saw that she and Lindsay were wearing the same color nail polish.

"How's your dad doing?" I asked.

"Fine."

"Fine," Lindsay echoed.

I swear, she was even beginning to *sound* like Jennifer.

"I thought he was really sick," I said.

"Oh, he was." She looked kind of sad saying it, but then she brightened up. "But he's all better. It's a miracle or something."

Lindsay said, "Isn't modern medicine amazing?"

The bell rang. Lindsay grabbed Jennifer's arm and pulled her into the classroom.

"Anyway, thanks for last night," Jennifer called out.

"No problem," I called back.

I swear I heard them giggling as soon as they were out of sight. What is it with girls and giggling? For that matter, what is it with girls?

All day, I kept thinking about the night before and Jennifer's dad's mysterious illness and Jennifer's even more mysterious behavior. I began to suspect that something was going on, like maybe she wasn't being totally honest with me. I guess I didn't want to believe it. Jennifer was so beautiful. How could anyone so beautiful not be honest?

Here's a lesson I should have learned then, but didn't figure out until later: Beautiful≠Honest.

Riding my bike to pick up Ben at his school that afternoon, I got to thinking. Here I was turning myself into Mr. Sensitivity and the champion baby-sitter of all time, and it was getting me nowhere with Jennifer. To make matters worse, I was spending all my afternoons with a seven year old whose greatest pleasure, except for climbing trees, was busting my chops.

I know, I know, you're going to remind me of what a good time we had the day before, putting that dinosaur kit together and making popcorn. Hey, don't get nostalgic on me. The way I figured, that was a one-time deal. Besides, I probably messed it up for life by running out the way I did.

When I picked Ben up, I was *sure* I had messed things up. He was hardly speaking to me. As happy as he'd been the day before, that's how miserable he was now. But it turned out his being miserable had nothing to do with me.

When we got back to his house, I found the dinosaur on the coffee table in the living room smashed to pieces. Next to it was a crumpled up piece of paper.

"What's this?" I asked, picking up the ball of paper. Ben grabbed it out of my hands and ran into the kitchen. I followed him.

"What's going on?" I asked. "What happened to the dinosaur?"

Wrong thing to say. "I don't care about that stupid dinosaur!" he snapped. "Don't talk to me about that stupid dinosaur!"

"Okay, okay," I said, backing off. He threw the crumpled paper across the room, slammed into a chair, and dropped his head onto his arms.

"So are you going to tell me what this is?" I asked, crossing the room and picking up the wad of paper.

He mumbled something that sounded like, "Leher-fru-ma-dud."

"What?"

Lifting his head, he looked me straight in the eye and spat out each word. "Letter. From. My. Dad."

"Oh."

"It came yesterday, but my mom didn't give it to me until this morning."

"Bad news?"

"You could say that. He promised I'd get to stay with him over Thanksgiving and now he says I can't. Okay?"

I guess I should have asked Ben first, but I uncrumpled the letter and read it. It had a real familiar ring.

"'Kiki wants us to go to her family's for Thanksgiving this year,'" I read aloud. "'I can't blame her. After all, some of her family haven't even met Colin yet. I know you might be disappointed, but I also know I can depend on a big guy like you to understand. Did you get the dinosaur kit I sent you? It's a triceratops, your favorite. See, I remember.'"

Without even asking, I knew who Kiki and Colin were. And I was willing to bet that the triceratops *wasn't* Ben's favorite dinosaur.

I pulled out a chair next to Ben and sat down. "*My* dad has pulled stuff like that," I told him.

He looked up at me, surprised. Wiping his nose with the back of his hand, he said, "Stuff like what?"

"Stuff like using his new wife and baby as an excuse for not having time for me. And sending me presents right before he's going to do something rotten so he wouldn't have to feel guilty."

"When did *your* dad leave?" Ben asked.

"Four years ago. It'll be five years next April. For a while, he lived in an apartment two blocks from our house. Then he moved to a town about ten miles from here. Now he lives in another state. I see him twice a year, but he keeps in touch by sending me pictures of my half sister and clothes that are too small."

"Don't you get mad?" Ben asked?

"Sometimes," I said. "But mostly I try not to think about it."

"Did you ever get so mad you wanted to run away?"

I nodded. "Oh yeah. In the beginning, I wanted to run away *all* the time. The problem was I could never figure out where I'd run to. When I was little I had a place."

Something in Ben's face changed. "What kind of place?" he asked.

Boy, I hadn't talked about this in a long time. "It wasn't much really," I told him, "just a place down at the end of my street where a bunch of bent-over trees came together and made a kind of fort. But it was *my* fort, and nobody knew about it but me and my best friend, Lucas. Of course, it's gone now. Has been for a long time. They put up houses."

Ben had this strange expression on his face. "What's the matter?" I asked.

"I have a place like that. It's not a fort, but it's mine. It even has a name. Florida."

"Florida," I said. "Right."

"Honest. You want to see it?"

"Sure," I said. "I'd like that."

"Follow me," he ordered, and took off through the back door.

I didn't know what to think when Ben led me through some woods not far from his house to the base of this gigantic tree.

"This is Florida?" I asked.

He nodded. "It's a tree house."

Looking up, I said, "I don't see it."

"Nobody can," Ben whispered, as if there was anybody around who could hear. "That's the best part."

He told me how he had discovered it one day when he was climbing trees in this part of the woods. "Somebody built it for their hiding place, I guess. But it must have been a long time ago, because I'm pretty sure I'm the only one who knows about it. So now it's my hiding place."

He clambered up, gesturing for me to follow.

I hated to let Ben down, but remember what I told you? I have this thing about heights. Still, for some reason, I really wanted to do it. I think maybe I needed a hiding place right about then myself. I just would have preferred one closer to the ground.

"What're you waiting for?" Ben shouted.

"Nothing," I called back. I took a deep breath and started to climb.

It took me a while, but I made it. Of course, by the time I'd pulled myself up onto the floor of the tree house, I thought I was going to be sick.

"What's the matter with you?" Ben asked. "Hey, you're not afraid of heights, are you?"

"No, I—"

"Yeah, you are."

"Okay. I am."

"No big deal," Ben said. "Just lie on your back and look up through the leaves. That's what I like to do."

I lay down. Next to my head was a plank with the word *Florida* written in big faded green letters. It must have come from an orange crate. Ben lay down, too, his head resting on *Florida*, inches from mine.

"Someday I want to climb this tree all the way to the top," Ben said. "It's the biggest, best tree in the whole world, even if it is old. And when I get to the top, know what I'm going to do? I'm going to build a new tree house, way up there in the sky, like it's floating, and nobody can see me, but I can see the whole world."

"Sounds good, Ben," I said. I meant it, too.

We got quiet then and stayed that way for a long time. Listening to the birds, watching the sunlight dance through the leaves, it didn't take long before all my problems began to fade away. Pretty soon, the only thing that mattered was being there.

"Ben," I whispered, "what's your favorite dinosaur?"

"Tyrannosaurus," he whispered back.

Chapter 8:
Barefoot Through a Valley of Vipers

Ben made me promise I wouldn't tell anybody about his secret place. I had to swear on a stack of his favorite comic books that if I ever broke my word I would walk barefoot through a valley of vipers. A valley of vipers. Those are Ben's words. Naturally, I agreed. I love that kind of stuff. It makes me feel like I'm seven again and Ben is Lucas. Everything changed between us after that. Ben was happy to see me when I showed up after school, and, as for basketball practice, well, he not only stopped complaining, he actually got interested.

One day in the locker room, he said, "I wish I could play like you."

That was the best thing he'd ever said to me. In fact, it was one of the best things *anybody* had ever said to me.

So the next afternoon I took him and a brand-new ball to the playground a few blocks from his house.

Typical Ben, or maybe just typical kid, he tossed the ball up in the air a few times in the general vicinity of the hoop, missed by a mile, and started beating himself up. "I stink!" he said in disgust.

"Come on, give yourself a break. Did anybody ever teach you to play?"

"No. My dad hated sports. And my mom's busy."

"So what do you expect?" I twirled the ball on the tip of my finger. "Basketball," I said, watching the ball spin, "is like . . . dancing."

Ben laughed.

"Okay, it sounds funny. But did you know that some of the pros take dance lessons to help them move around the floor? It's true. Look, you've got to get past the opposition, right?"

Ben shrugged. "I guess."

"So how do you do that? *Moves*, my man. Cool moves. Come on, get the ball away from me."

I dribbled so close to Ben I practically handed him the ball. He lunged at me. Pivoting and changing hands, I maneuvered my way out; Ben almost landed on his face. "Save that move for football!" I shouted as I dribbled away and drove to the hoop. I went in for a lay-up.

I missed.

"I meant to do that," I said, turning to Ben.

"Yeah, right. Cool move, Nick."

Grabbing the ball, I said, "Okay, let me show you what I can do when I'm serious. Watch the wrist action." This time I sank the ball.

"Awesome!" Ben said.

I smiled and passed the ball to Ben, motioning him to the lower hoop nearby. "Your turn," I said. "And don't worry about making the basket, okay? We're working on delivery here."

As I was helping Ben get the feel of the ball in his hands, he said, "Nick, can I go with you to the game tomorrow night?"

"You want to?" I asked, surprised. "It's just an exhibition game against Emerson."

"I know. But I want to see if you're any good in a real game. So can I?"

"Sure," I told him. "I'll clear it with your mom."

He looked up at the hoop then, positioned the ball, and let it fly. The ball soared through the air and landed with a soft *swoosh* in the center of the hoop. "All *right!*" I said, slapping him five.

Ben looked about the happiest I'd ever seen him.

"Can I keep practicing?" he asked, running to retrieve the ball.

I noticed Kelly walking in our direction, and I waved. "You'd better," I told him. "That ball cost good money. I don't want to see you wasting it."

"You mean . . . "

"It's yours," I told him, "if you want it."

"Awesome!" Ben said for the second time that day.

"Since when do you play basketball?" Kelly called out to Ben.

He looked a little embarrassed. "Since . . ." he said with a nod in my direction. Then to both of us he said, "Can I practice without you guys watching me?"

"No sweat," I told him. "Just remember, keep the wrist loose and the moves cool."

"Okay, coach!" Ben shouted, as he dribbled away.

"So Kelly," I said as we moved toward the swings, "I haven't seen you in a while."

"I've been practically living at my friend Emma's," she told me. "We're working on this major science project. It's been fun, but we're both wiped out."

Glancing back at Ben, she asked, "What's going on with you two?"

"Progress," I said simply. I didn't want to tell her too much; after all, there *was* that walk through the valley of vipers at stake.

"I can see that," she said. "But how did it happen? I mean, I don't see you guys for a week and suddenly you're best buds."

"Best *buds*?" I said. "Where'd you hear that?"

Kelly blushed, as we sat down on adjoining swings. "TV, okay?"

"Well, I don't know about us being 'best buds,'" I

said, "but it turns out we have a lot in common. And Ben decided he liked basketball."

"So you're teaching him."

"Yep."

Kelly fell silent, then said, "I think you're going to be good for Ben. I've never . . ."

"What?" I asked when she didn't finish her sentence.

"I was just going to say I've never known a boy like you."

I hoped she meant that as a compliment. She was looking down at her feet when she said it, and the way her hair fell over her face I couldn't tell for sure. But I had the feeling she did. The neat thing about Kelly was that she was so honest.

At that moment, I was feeling anything but. I mean, here was this nice girl thinking I was this nice guy who actually *liked* to baby-sit. I wasn't sure why, but I had to tell her the truth.

"Kelly," I said, "I need to tell you something. It's a little embarrassing, but I could use some advice. Girl-type advice."

Kelly lifted her head and looked at me. I thought maybe she was annoyed or something, but then she said, "I guess I qualify as a girl-type. Go ahead."

So I took a deep breath and told her everything. Mitch, Jennifer, the bet, even the tutu at halftime . . .

"Whose brilliant idea was that?" she asked.

"Mine."

She laughed and shook her head. "So let me get this straight," she said. "You're baby-sitting because of a girl."

"Not exactly. I didn't know I was going to have to baby-sit when I signed up for the class. See, I figured Jennifer would be impressed when she saw what a sensitive guy I was. Now I'm not so sure. To tell you the truth, I don't know if I even care anymore."

"Really?" Kelly asked.

I nodded. "But I've *got* to beat Mitch. My whole life Mitch has one-upped me. This time I really thought I could win." I dug my heels into the sand below the swings and watched Ben chasing the ball around the basketball court in the distance.

"Not that I really care what you do," Kelly said, "but if you want to win, it sounds to me like you need to try a different approach with Jennifer. She isn't what you'd call the liberated type. I think you should do something really old-fashioned and romantic. Like dinner."

"I can't ask her out on a date," I reminded her.

"You don't have to. Can you cook?"

I gave Kelly a look. "I'm fourteen," I said.

"So?" Kelly gave me a look of her own. It was kind of mischievous. I liked it. I listened. And before I left that playground, I had an amazing plan of action. Now all I had to do was figure out how to pull it off.

"Pooch," I said that night after dinner. My cat was bathing himself in the light of the television set. Every once in a while he'd give his tongue a rest and look up at me as if he were listening. "What do you think of the idea of cooking dinner to impress a girl? I mean, not a regular dinner. No pizza or hamburgers, but I don't know, pasta, maybe. And real vegetables. And that kind of bread that's as long as a baseball bat. And candlelight. And some sort of fancy dessert, like . . ."

Pooch brought up a hair ball.

"You're becoming a truly lousy conversationalist," I said.

At least Pooch listened, which is more than I could say for Lucas. I tried calling him that night. He was out, his mother told me, at Michelle's house. The next day he didn't even come by to pick me up for school. When I got there, he was hanging out by Michelle's locker, playing his harmonica for her. They were both wearing these new hats that were about as goofy as the way they looked at each other.

Michelle saw me first and waved hi. Lucas waved, too, as if he sort of kind of knew who I was. Lucas, I could see, was going to be as useless to me as Pooch.

The trouble was, that night I really needed a friend. Okay, so it wasn't a big-deal game. But there were all these people there I wanted to impress. My mom. Ben. His mom. Kelly. Jennifer.

I know it shouldn't have mattered, but I wanted to show Jennifer I could play basketball better than Mitch. Which was pretty dumb on my part, because if there's one thing Mitch is definitely better at than me, it's sports. He's also more ruthless.

Do I need to tell you what happened? It was seventh grade all over again. There we were, last quarter, score tied, the crowd going wild. I had the ball, I fumbled, Mitch got the ball away from me, he scored. The buzzer sounded. The game was over.

The last thing I remember seeing before heading for the locker room was Jennifer running across the court and throwing her arms around Mitch.

Lucas showed up for a few minutes while I was getting dressed. "Tough going," he said, punching me lightly on the arm. Then as he was leaving he said, "Guess what? Michelle asked me to the Vice-Versa Dance!"

So much for a friend in need.

I waited until everyone else had left the locker room before picking up my gym bag and heading for the door. I was hoping my mom had been smart enough to know I wanted to walk home alone. I didn't want to have to face anybody.

But there were two people waiting for me.

Ben. And Kelly.

We didn't talk much as we walked back to my house, where Ben's mom was waiting. But when we were almost at my front door, Ben said, "I'm glad I came. Now I know you're really good and not just a lot of talk."

"We saw how Mitch got the ball away from you," Kelly added. "And you know what I think? I think you're right. You've *got* to beat him, Nick."

I looked at Kelly, then at Ben. "Cool moves, you guys," I said.

We went inside then and ate ice cream with hot fudge sauce as if there was something to celebrate. And maybe there was.

Chapter 9:

Still in the Game

The Vice-Versa Dance was a week away. Michelle had asked Lucas. Lindsay had asked Augie. Jennifer hadn't asked anybody.

The morning after the game with Emerson, I overheard Mitch complaining to Augie about it. "I don't get it," he said. "What's Jennifer's problem?" Like any girl who wasn't in love with him had a problem.

Of course, I have to admit I wondered the same thing. I mean, when I saw Jennifer throw her arms around Mitch after the game, I figured I might as well go out and get myself fitted for a tutu. But she still hadn't asked him to the dance.

So I was still in the game.

I was beginning to think my romantic dinner for two just might do the trick. The best part was that the night before, at my house after the game, Mrs. Coburn asked me if the next time I sat for Ben I could stay late and *make dinner*. I could hardly believe my luck. I said yes before my mother had a chance to open her mouth.

See, there were a couple of little problems: 1) the only time I had tried cooking was once on Mother's Day, and that's the reason my mom has said, "Let's go to a restaurant this year," every Mother's Day since, and 2) I had no idea how I would get Jennifer to come to Ben's house.

The way I looked at it, problem number one took a few simple recipes and a trip to the supermarket. As for problem number two, all I had to do was wait for a solution to present itself. And it did—in Baby-sitting and Child Care 101.

By the time fifth period rolled around, Lucas and I were back to our old selves. We'd worked it all out that morning, walking to school. I told him I thought he was acting like a jerk because of Michelle. He said Jennifer was making a fool out of me. I swung my gym bag at him. He hit me with his hat. And after that, everything was cool.

So there we were, Lucas and I, up to our elbows in suds, giving this baby a bath, when the next brilliant idea struck.

"Check Jennifer out," I said out of the corner of my mouth.

Lucas looked across the room. Everybody in the class was working in teams, learning how to bathe real

babies in real water in real plastic tubs. Under the circumstances, I thought the adults who'd brought the
babies in looked remarkably calm. Anyway, the only
one not getting soaked by a kicking, splashing baby
was Jennifer. No, she was sitting with her back to
everyone else writing in that flower-covered book of
hers. "How does she get away with it?" Lucas asked.

"Oh, Jennifer," Ms. Marlowe called out over the
din. "You feel like joining us?"

Jennifer looked up. "Do I have to get my hands
wet?" she asked.

"Yes, you do," said Ms. Marlowe.

Jennifer sighed, closed her book, and snapped it
shut. I noticed that she locked it with a tiny key.

"It's a diary," I whispered to Lucas.

"So?"

"So I just figured out the perfect way to get
Jennifer to come over to Ben's tonight. Cover for me."

Wiping my hands on my pants, I watched Jennifer
cross the room and dip the tips of her fingernails into
Michelle's baby tub. Michelle flicked some sudsy water
on her, which made Michelle laugh and Jennifer cry,
"Stop it, Michelle!"

It was just the diversion I needed. Quickly, I made
my way across the room and, making sure no one but
Lucas was looking, swept Jennifer's diary off her desk
and into my back pocket.

"I can't believe you did that," Lucas said when I got back.

"All's fair in love and war," I retorted.

"Yes, but—"

"Listen, Lucas, love has made you put on the dumbest hats I've ever seen, not to mention serenade Michelle with your harmonica in public places, so I wouldn't talk if I were you."

He didn't. He shoved a soapy baby at me instead.

Getting stuff out of my locker at the end of the day, I noticed Jennifer going crazy searching her locker for the lost diary. Lindsay was hovering nearby, fluffing her imitation Jennifer haircut with her imitation Jennifer nails.

"I thought you said you had it in class," Lindsay was saying.

"I told you, I looked there a million times, okay?" Jennifer slammed her locker door. "I've got to find it, Lindsay. Do you have any idea the kinds of things I've written in there?"

"Oh, I'll bet it's fabulous," Lindsay said breathlessly. "Could I read it sometime, Jen?"

"No, you could not," Jennifer snapped.

"Oh, well, don't worry. It'll show up."

"It better," Jennifer said.

I chuckled to myself as the two of them walked away. Oh, this new Nick Kramer was one sly devil.

Of course, there *was* dinner to contend with. Believe me, I thought about ordering takeout and pretending I'd cooked it, but I knew I wouldn't be able to fool anyone as sophisticated as Jennifer. Unfortunately, Lucas had to baby-sit and Kelly wasn't going to be around until later in the evening, so it was up to Ben and me to pull it off.

Ben really got into it, although I had to veto a few of his menu suggestions. Anyway, here—with a little help from my French book and a menu from an Italian restaurant we found in the kitchen—is what we finally decided on:

Menu for Romantic Dinner for Two
Appetizer
Les cochons en couvertures (pigs in blankets)
Main Course
Salade (salad)
Fettuccine con polpette (spaghetti with meatballs)
Les haricots verts (string beans)
Dessert
Gâteau chocolat (chocolate cake)
Beverage
Grape soda

I chose grape soda because Jennifer wore a lot of purple; I figured it was her favorite color.

Coming up with the menu was pretty easy.

Preparing it was, as my dad used to say, a horse of a different color. Don't ask me what it means.

While Ben was working on the meatballs, I put the rest of the plan into action. First, I called Jennifer, who was pleased to know I'd found her diary. Sort of.

"Did you *read* it?" she asked with an edge so sharp you could have sliced cheese with it. "Because if you read even one little word, I'll . . . I'll braid your nose hairs!"

Wow. I had no idea Jennifer was so creative. For the first time, I actually wanted to read her diary.

"Of course I didn't read it," I said. "I just found it in class and—"

"Well, I want it back. Now."

"One-two cup of bread crumbs," I heard Ben muttering in the background. "Twelve cups of bread crumbs."

"I can't bring it to your house," I told Jennifer. "I'm baby-sitting. Maybe you could come over to Ben's."

"Where does he live? I'll be right there."

"No!" I cried, glancing at the clock. It was a little before five. "I'm not here now. I mean, I'm not there. I'm . . . I'm calling from a pay phone. How about six?"

There was a long pause. I held my breath. Please say yes. Please.

"Oh, fine. But I'm telling you, Nick Kramer, if it looks like one page has been touched . . ."

"I know. Nose hairs. See you at six."

I can't say the conversation was exactly encouraging, but that didn't stop me from having fantasies.

I've come for my diary.

I have it inside. Can't you stay for a moment?

Well, just a moment. Why, Nick, this table . . . fine china, crystal goblets, candlelight! Is that, yes, it's grape soda! How did you know it was my favorite?

It had to be. It's purple, the color of passion.

"Nick!" I was jarred out of my reverie by the sight of Ben holding what looked like a melting basketball in his hands. "I don't know," he said, "this is the biggest meatball I ever saw! I used twelve cups of bread crumbs like the recipe said, but—"

I looked at the cookbook. "That's one-half cup, Ben. One slash two. One-half, not twelve!"

"Oh."

I took a deep breath. "Never mind. The meatballs will have a little extra bread in them, that's all. We've got a lot more to take care of before she gets here. The cake, we'd better get the cake in the oven."

Now, let me ask you something about eggs. If I said to you, "Separate two eggs and fold the whites into the batter," would you know what I was talking about? I mean, who writes these cookbooks? Personally, my guess is that it's the same people who write computer manuals. I did finally figure out that separating two eggs didn't mean making them sit on opposite sides of the room. It means getting the yolks and the white stuff apart.

That's a trick I'm not sure even Houdini could have pulled off.

It took me the entire box of one dozen eggs to get two separated. And even then there were some pieces of eggshell that made it into the batter. *Folding* just means "mixing in." Why couldn't they say so?

Anyway, while I was folding I went back to my fantasy.

Nick, did you plan all this? I'm beginning to think you took my diary just to get me here.

Would you be angry with me if I did?

How could I be angry with someone who went to all this trouble just for me? Flowers, music, pigs in blankets.

A buzzer sounded somewhere. At first, I thought it was the doorbell. Panic was about to overtake me when I realized it was the oven timer. I'd set it so I'd know when to put the spaghetti in the pot.

"Find a pot for the spaghetti!" I shouted to Ben as I shoved the cake in the oven. I don't know, it sure didn't look like any cake my mom had ever made.

"Aye, aye, Captain!" Ben called back. He ducked his head into a cupboard and came back out with this big pot with a funny-looking knob on top. "How's this?" he asked.

"Looks fine," I said. "What's that thing on top for?"

"Beats me."

"Never mind. Just put in the spaghetti and get the water boiling."

As I was setting the dining-room table, Jennifer returned to my thoughts. I could just picture her sitting there, wiping her mouth daintily on a fine linen napkin after enjoying a piece of the best chocolate cake she'd ever eaten, reaching out her hand to mine . . .

Oh, Nick, Mitch would never have done anything like this. He's so, so . . .

Macho?

Yes, and you're so, so . . .

Sensitive?

Yes. What a fool I've been not to see it before. Nick, will you go with me to the Vice-Versa Dance? Please, Nick, say yes. Please, Nick. Nick . . .

"Nick!"

Ben's urgent cry got me back into the kitchen, pronto. I couldn't believe my eyes. Ben was pulling a tray of these disgusting little black things out of the microwave ("Hope she likes her pigs in blankets well done," he said), while smoke filled the oven and water bubbled over the top of the spaghetti pot and onto the floor. I yanked open the oven door, setting off the smoke alarm in the process. Turning the burner down under the spaghetti, I secured the top on the pot and yelled for Ben to turn off the blender, which for some

reason was his appliance of choice for making tomato
sauce.

"It's the doorbell," Ben sang out over all the
racket.

"It's the smoke alarm," I called back, dropping the
cake on the floor. A thin dish towel is not a substitute
for a pot holder.

"It's the doorbell *and* the smoke alarm."

"It can't be. It's only . . .' I glanced at the clock.
"Six."

This time I heard the doorbell. I looked around.
The kitchen was a disaster zone. The table was half
set. I was wearing an apron covered with so many
stains I looked like I'd just performed major surgery.

"Get the candles!" I commanded Ben as I dashed
for the front door.

Jennifer was leaning on the bell on the other side.
I stopped, caught my breath, patted down my cowlicks, counted to three, and swung the door wide open.

"Well, hi there," I said to Jennifer, trying to sound
casual. Jennifer couldn't take her eyes off my apron.

"Where's my diary?" she asked.

I inhaled deeply and looked at Jennifer with what
I hoped was an impossible combination of manly
charm and magnetic force.

"I have it inside," I said. "Can't you stay for a
moment?"

"What for?"

"Well, I have a little dinner prepared and I thought—"

I never got to finish my sentence. There was loud BOOM! from the kitchen.

"What was *that*?" Jennifer asked.

"Ben!" I cried.

I ran to the kitchen as fast as I could, not knowing what I'd find when I got there.

Chapter 10:
A Miracle or What?

Ben was covered in spaghetti. He looked amazingly calm under the circumstances. I couldn't say the same for Jennifer.

"The pot exploded," Ben explained, sucking a strand of the wayward pasta into his mouth.

Jennifer's eyes were about twice their normal size. "What are you guys *doing* in here?" she asked. Totally humiliated, I watched as she scanned the scene: piles of dirty dishes, spilled flour and eggs and milk, a cake (sort of) lying upside down on the floor, spaghetti hanging everywhere like some kind of Italian Spanish moss. And there was Ben in the center of it all, sucking spaghetti and looking like he'd been through a war. "I think you were better off in the cellar," she told him.

I laughed in self-defense. "Great sense of humor," I said to Jennifer.

"I wasn't joking."

"Yes, well, seriously, we were making spaghetti."

"In a pressure cooker? You can't cook spaghetti in a pressure cooker!"

"Oh, is that what that is?"

Jennifer glared at me.

"Care to stay for dinner?" I asked.

I'll never know what her answer might have been, for Ben, bless his well-intentioned little heart, chose that very moment to check the progress of the tomato sauce, which was whirling wildly in the blender. Unfortunately, it did not occur to him to hit the off button before lifting the lid.

Jennifer screamed as the first barrage of tomato sauce hit her. I was too shocked to open my mouth.

Ben wasn't. He was dripping with the stuff, but that didn't stop him from licking his lips and proclaiming, "*Delizioso! Molto delizioso!*"

"Towel!" Jennifer commanded. I obeyed.

"Diary!" she snapped after using the towel to wipe her hands and clear her face of enough tomato sauce so that she could see.

I slunk over to the silverware drawer and removed the diary. She snatched it out of my hands.

"Maybe you'd like a little grape soda to cut the tomato taste?" I suggested weakly. She was already out of the kitchen and halfway through the front door.

Watching her go, I called out, "Is that a *no*?" My

mother says I have my father's persistence. She doesn't mean it as a compliment. I guess I just wanted to believe I still had a chance with Jennifer, even though I knew I had just blown it—big-time.

Returning to the kitchen, I found Ben sitting on a stool at the counter, a plate of spaghetti and tomato sauce in front of him and a piece of cake in one hand. "I know you're going to find this hard to believe," he said, "but when you dip the cake in the tomato sauce, it isn't half bad."

Blame it on my state of mind. I tried it. It wasn't half bad.

The next day was Saturday. There were six days until the Vice-Versa Dance. It hit me at breakfast that not only hadn't Jennifer asked me, neither had anybody else.

"Pooch," I said, slipping him a piece of my cinnamon toast—Pooch has always had a taste for cinnamon toast, although it makes him sneeze even more than usual—"I can understand why Jennifer doesn't like me. She thinks I keep a seven year old locked in his cellar except when I bring him up to pull off sneak attacks with tomato sauce. She's probably decided I'm a total psycho. So much for Mr. Sensitivity.

"But what about other girls? I mean, even Lucas has a date for the dance. Lucas! Up to this year, his idea of conversation with a girl was, 'Get out of the way.'" I sighed. Pooch looked up at me with soulful eyes and, showing true compassion for the depth of my despair, held off a good ten seconds before sneezing cinnamon and sugar all over my foot.

Lucas called at around eleven. "My dad's taking me to the mall to get some clothes for the dance," he said. "Want to come?"

I thought about watching Lucas—and probably a whole bunch of other kids from school—pick out clothes for a dance I hadn't been invited to. What did I have to lose? Only the tiny shred of self-respect I had left.

"Sure," I told him.

The way things turned out, it was good I went.

I was right about one thing. There were a lot of other kids from school at the mall. "This place is *happenin'*," Lucas said enthusiastically, after his dad dropped us off and told us where to meet him in an hour.

"*Happenin'*?" I asked. This was not Lucasspeak. "Has an alien from the in-crowd taken over your vocabulary?"

Lucas laughed. "You know what your problem is, Nick? You need to get over it and cheer up. Jennifer was bad news from the beginning. It's too bad Julianne Barberetto moved," he said. "I'll bet you would have worn her down by now. She would have asked you to the dance."

That cheered me up, all right.

To my surprise, Lucas really got into shopping for

clothes. I'm talking about clothes that were actually new and not from a thrift store and that looked like clothes normal kids wore. He tried to get me to buy something, too.

"Somebody could still ask you," he kept saying. "You should be prepared." I didn't tell him that I had enough new clothes left over from my summer shopping spree to be prepared if *five* girls asked me. Which at that point was about as likely as *one* girl asking me.

Besides, I was hardly in the mood to try on clothes. After a while, I decided to hang out in front of the store where Lucas was currently keeping the sales staff and changing room occupied. That was when the miracle started to happen.

There I was, sitting on this bench trying to decide whether to have a chili-and-guacamole stuffed baked potato or the World's Largest Chocolate Chip Cookie for lunch, when who do I see across the mall walking from one direction but Jennifer and Lindsay? And who's coming from the other direction but Mitch and Augie? When they got together, they stopped and began talking. They were too far away for me to hear anything, but I had a perfect view. It was sort of like watching a movie with the sound off.

At first, it looked like Mitch was doing his usual Mr. Charm number on Jennifer, and she was doing her usual twirling-her-fingers-in-her-hair number on him. Then Augie and Lindsay did a lot of talking, with Augie shoving Mitch in this go-ahead-you-can-do-it kind of way. Mitch had his head down, looking almost—hard as it was to believe—shy. Finally, he shrugged and opened his mouth to say something, but stopped when he turned and saw me sitting there. All of a sudden, he got all flustered. He turned back real fast—I don't think anybody noticed that he saw me—and started shrugging his shoulders and bobbing his head around like a total fool.

I'm not sure what happened next because Lucas came out of the store with these two huge shopping bags and said, "Let's go to the food court. I'm in the mood for burritos and fried rice."

Okay, now I'm closing in on the miracle.

To get to the food court we had to cross the center of the mall and walk right through where Mitch and Augie and Jennifer and Lindsay were hanging out. Only now they weren't just hanging out. Something had happened.

Jennifer had her hands on her hips and was really giving it to Mitch.

"Whoa, what's going on?" Lucas asked when he saw them.

We could hear Jennifer's voice but not her words. Mitch had his hands up in front of him as if he was saying, "Okay, okay. Back off." Then Jennifer must have said something really shocking because Lindsay's jaw dropped like it was going to hit the floor and Mitch and Augie looked speechless. Augie doesn't always have an easy time thinking of words, so the expression looked normal on him, but on Mitch it was a horse of a different color. Don't ask.

Okay, here's the miracle. Lucas and I are almost there. Jennifer has her back to us. She's saying, "I mean it, too!" She turns and bumps right into me.

"Nick!" she says, surprised. Then she gets this strange smile on her face, and with a glance over her shoulder she adds some sugar to her voice and says again, "Nick . . ."

"Yeah?" I say, having no idea what's coming next.

"Would you like to go with me to the Vice-Versa Dance?"

Now is that a miracle or what?

Chapter 11:

Girls Are Very Confusing

The next week at school, Jennifer acted like a different person with me. She smiled at me and twirled her fingers in her hair, and when I said something funny she laughed instead of rolling her eyes. She laughed loudest whenever Mitch was around.

"See?" I told Lucas one day in baby-sitting class. "I was right all along—Jennifer *does* like me."

Lucas didn't say anything. He just nodded his head the way my mother does when she thinks she's right and I'm wrong but she doesn't want to talk about it. I hate that.

I didn't push it with Lucas, though. Even I knew there was too much that didn't make sense. I mean, the girl who had asked me to the dance was the same girl who had been ready to kill me the night before for coating her in tomato sauce.

But, hey, I wasn't about to look a gift horse in the

mouth. That's another thing my dad used to say; he must have had horses on the brain. The way I saw it, the most beautiful girl in the school had asked me to the dance and she *hadn't* asked Mitch. I'd beaten him at last! To be honest, it was even more fun picturing Mitch dancing in his tutu than me dancing with Jennifer.

I couldn't wait to tell Kelly the good news. The problem was that she was hardly around that week; her science project had been chosen to go to a state competition, so she and her friend were working hard to make it even better. As it turned out I didn't get a chance to tell her until Friday afternoon when the dance was only a few hours away.

We were sitting in Ben's kitchen while he was in the next room juggling rolled-up socks.

"You won the bet?" Kelly asked. "She really asked you?"

Kelly's face was never easy to read, but this time it may as well have been written in another language. I couldn't tell if she was happy for me or surprised or angry or upset or she didn't care at all. Or all of the above. Girls are very confusing. If you don't believe me, wait'll I tell you what happened next.

"Yeah," I said, "it's really amazing. And today she gave me this."

I handed her a note Jennifer had passed to me in school.

"Dear Nick," Kelly read aloud, "I can't wait until tonight. ♥, Jen."

Of course, she didn't say "♥"; she said "heart shape."

"When did she give you this?" Kelly asked, handing it back to me.

"Between classes. Right in front of Mitch and everything. You should have been there to see the look on his face. It was so cool."

"Oh. She gave it to you in front of Mitch?"

"Yeah. Oh, listen, I wanted to ask you something."

"More advice?"

"Huh?"

"Never mind. Just ask."

"It's about flowers," I said. "Do you think she'd like white roses or red roses better? My mom said red roses are classic, whatever that means, but Jennifer told me she's wearing a black-and-white dress, so I thought—"

"White." Kelly practically spat the word at me.

"Uh, okay," I said. "Oh, there's one other thing—"

Kelly stood up suddenly, knocking over her chair. "What? You want me to tell you what to wear? Teach you how to dance? What?"

"I was just asking for some advice. Listen, Kelly, you've been a big help to me. I don't know what I would have done if—"

"Oh, that makes me feel a lot better, Nick." You could have cut the sarcasm with a knife.

"Well, you don't have to get so mad," I said. "I'm just nervous, is all. I don't know how to act around a beautiful girl."

Bad move.

"Okay, that's it!" Kelly cried, her cheeks looking like they might burst into flame any second. "Nick Kramer, you are one colossal *jerk*!"

I turned to see if Ben was listening. I detected some movement at the dining-room door.

"I'm sorry," I said, not knowing what I was apologizing for, but lowering my voice so that maybe Kelly would lower hers. I didn't want Ben to hear us. It reminded me of all the times I'd been alone in one room listening to my parents fighting in another.

"You know what your problem is?" Kelly went on loudly. "Your problem is that you only think about yourself. It never occurred to you how I might feel being your little helper, giving you advice all the time. And what about Ben?"

"What about him?" I asked, glancing nervously at the open door.

"Now that you've put in your thirty hours for baby-sitting class and won your stupid bet, you'll drop him like a hot potato. Tell the truth, Nick, do you *enjoy* spending every afternoon hanging out with a seven year old?"

Kelly wasn't giving me time to think. "Gee, I—"

"I thought you were so cool wanting to be a baby-sitter. Ben even thought you liked him. Well, I guess the joke's on us."

Looking at the clock, she said, "You'd better leave, Nick. You only have three hours to get ready for your date."

She looked like she was going to cry. "Just get out of here, okay?" she said, her voice shaking a little. "I'll take care of Ben. I'll tell his mother you had more important things to do. Just go."

I didn't know what else to do. I turned and went out through the dining room, hoping to say good-bye to Ben, but as soon as I got there he ran up the stairs and slammed his bedroom door.

"Tell him I'll see him Monday," I said to Kelly.

She didn't answer. She was halfway up the stairs after Ben.

I left, feeling like somebody had taken the new Nick Kramer, stuffed him inside a football, and kicked him clear out of the stadium. I stood on the sidewalk in front of Ben's house, wondering where I'd land.

A few hours later when I landed at Jennifer's house, I was still feeling like that football, but at the same time I felt like the captain of the team. What can I say? Going with Jennifer to my first high school dance was a pretty major thing, even though I had this nagging feeling I might have lost Kelly and Ben because of it.

Although it was girl-ask-boy, Jennifer told me that one of her rules was that the boy always picked up the girl—even if, as in my case, it was the boy's mom who did the driving. I made my mom promise to wait in the car while I went inside to get Jennifer and not to make any cracks about how grown-up I was or what a cute couple we made when we came back. She said she'd try.

As I was standing on the front steps of Jennifer's house, she called out, "Stand up straight!" Mothers.

Jennifer's house was really big, and I could tell from the way her parents had fixed it up that they had a lot of money. Her mom and dad looked like they had stepped out of the pages of a magazine, same as their furniture. I pegged Mr. Edwards as a former football player, and it was a safe bet that Mrs. Edwards had once been a cheerleader. They were still pretty rah-rah, if you know what I mean. Mr. Edwards grabbed my hand as if handshaking were an Olympic event and he was going for the gold. Mrs. Edwards presented her hand as if it were a gift. I wasn't sure what to do with it, but I couldn't help noticing the monster diamond on one finger. I said, "Nice ring." She looked surprised and pleased at the same time.

"Why, thank you," she said in a voice too high for her age.

Mr. Edwards gave me a conspiratorial wink. "Jennifer will be down in a few minutes," he said. "You know girls." His wife giggled. I don't know if it was my imagination or not, but the air seemed to be getting thinner. All I wanted to do was sit down.

Luckily, Jennifer's foot appeared at the top of the stairs. She came down slowly, step by step, as if she were a bride or was just learning how to use stairs or something. Out of the corner of my eye, I noticed that Mr. and Mrs. Edwards seemed to have stopped breathing. They were watching their daughter descend the stairs as if they were witnessing history in the making.

When Jennifer came into full view, I have to admit *my* breath stopped for a few seconds there, too. I had no idea fourteen-year-old girls could look like that. The only thing that spoiled the moment was the thought that Mitch Buckley wouldn't be at the dance to see me come in with this—hey, there's no other word for it— goddess on my arm.

When she reached the bottom step, she just stood there. I felt like she was waiting for us to applaud or something. I don't know, maybe we would have, but the phone rang just then and broke the mood.

"Here," I said, handing Jennifer her corsage as her father went to answer the phone.

Jennifer smiled. I melted. "White roses," she said. "How perfect."

Perfect was the perfect word for how I felt as Jennifer put on her corsage and said, "Shall we go?"

She and her mother kissed good-bye—actually,

they kissed the air on either side of their cheeks—and we were all set to leave when Mr. Edwards returned to the room, a puzzled look on his face, and said, "Nick, it's for you."

"What's for me?"

"The phone."

Jennifer responded before I could. "This is totally bizarre, Nick," she said. "Why would anybody be calling you at *my* house?"

"It's a girl," her father said. "Kelly, I think her name was. She sounded very upset."

"Kelly?" I said.

"Who's Kelly?" said Jennifer.

As I followed Mr. Edwards into the kitchen, I heard Jennifer and her mom going on about the mysterious caller.

"Kelly?" "Who's Kelly?" "Do you know this girl, dear?" "Does it seem like I know her?" "Well, who is she?" "How should I know?" "You're sure her name is Kelly?" "I *told* you, I don't know her!" "Well, then, why is she calling here?"

"Kelly?" I said into the phone.

"I'm sorry to bother you on your *date*, Nick, but Ben's missing."

"What do you mean?" I asked.

"I think he ran away. His mom and I have looked all over and can't find him. I thought you might know where he's gone."

Jennifer appeared in the doorway of the kitchen. "I'm ready," she said.

I nodded in her direction.

"Nick?" Kelly said. "Are you there?"

I nodded at the phone. "Yeah, I—"

"Ben was really upset after you left this afternoon," Kelly went on. "I think he heard us talking."

My stomach sank. I thought about all the times I'd heard my parents talking, how I'd wanted to run away, too. Sometimes I did run away—and always to the same place. That's when it hit me.

"I know where Ben is," I told Kelly.

Jennifer cleared her throat. "I'm *ready*," she repeated.

I looked at her. The goddess of the freshman class of Calvin Coolidge High. I couldn't believe I was about to do what I was about to do.

"Kelly," I said into the phone, "I'll be right over."

I don't know which of the three of us was the most shocked. I couldn't see Kelly's face but Jennifer's definitely gave her the lead.

"But your date," Kelly said. "What about the bet? It was so important to you."

"I'll *be* there," I told Kelly. "Wait for me at Ben's."

I hung up the phone and swallowed hard. "Um, Jennifer, something has sort of come up," I said.

"It had better be a matter of life or death," she snarled.

I didn't care for her tone. It was funny how in a matter of seconds she no longer looked so goddess-like. "Well," I told her, "it's not like the time your dad was so sick. He sure looks healthy now, by the way." I think I actually saw her blush. "But it *is* important. Will you wait for me?"

Jennifer recovered quickly from her brush with humility. "Don't count on it," she said.

"Emergency," I told her parents on the way out. "Sorry. I still like your ring, Mrs. Edwards. And Mr. Edwards, I . . . I . . . that's a great sweater."

I don't think they knew what to say. Who could blame them? Jennifer wasn't the kind of girl any guy in his right mind would walk out on. At least, that's what they thought. Personally, I wasn't so sure anymore.

All I knew at that moment was that Ben needed me. And I needed to find him.

Chapter 12:

And You Know Something? I Did

"Stop worrying," I told my mother for the tenth time.

"I can't help it," she said, turning our car down Ben's street. "That poor girl thought she was going to the dance with you, and you just left her there."

"Hey, Mom, that 'poor girl' was probably on the phone to Mitch before I was out the door. Jennifer can take care of herself."

My mother sighed and shook her head.

"Besides," I reminded her before she had a chance to start in about how different kids are from when she was growing up, "Ben's the one you should be worrying about."

"True," my mother admitted.

Kelly and Mrs. Coburn were waiting for us at the curb when we arrived.

"We'll need flashlights," I told them as I jumped out of the car.

"Where are we going?" Mrs. Coburn asked.

"To Florida."

"*Florida*?"

But Ben wasn't in Florida as I'd expected; he was above it. *High* above it. The little monkey had climbed almost to the top of his favorite tree.

I couldn't see him at first, but I could hear him calling. "Help! Up here!"

"Ben!" I shouted.

"Nick! I can't move!"

Mrs. Coburn gasped. "Are you hurt?" she yelled.

"No, but I'm stuck between these two branches, and one of them feels a little shaky."

"Don't try to move!" I yelled.

"I'll call 911," my mother told Mrs. Coburn. "You wait here with the kids."

"Thank you," Mrs. Coburn said, "I—"

A loud *crack* cut off her sentence.

"Ben!" she screamed.

We heard Ben crying.

"Are you okay, Ben?" I called out. I couldn't make him out with my flashlight.

"I think this part of the tree is dead, Nick. Nick, get me down from here! Please, Nick . . ."

I hadn't noticed before but Kelly was holding on to my arm. "Can you get him down?" she asked.

I looked up and tried to decide whether tree climbing would be any easier in the dark. The answer was simple: dark, light, or blindfolded, this was going to be the hardest thing I'd ever had to do. But what choice did I have?

"Nick!" Ben called out. "I'm scared!"

Scared wasn't a word in Ben's vocabulary. "Hang in there, Ben!" I shouted. "I'm coming up!"

Kelly squeezed my arm. "Good luck," she said.

"Thanks. I'll need it."

While my mom ran to call 911, Kelly and Mrs. Coburn kept the beams of their flashlights trained on the tree just above me. I was carrying another small flashlight in my mouth. I thought, All I need now is to take up juggling and I can be a regular one-man circus. You might not believe I actually thought that, but I did. I often have these weird thoughts when I'm terrified. It helps keep other thoughts away. Thoughts about stuff like falling, breaking bones, dying. Stuff like that.

About halfway up, I decided that the darkness definitely helped. The only bad part was that I couldn't see where Ben was exactly, and I had no idea how hard it was going to be to disentangle him from the tree once I got there. I kept calling out, "Hang on, Little Monkey. I'm coming. You'll be all right." And to myself, I said, "Cool moves, Nick. You can do it. You can do it."

Then all of a sudden this amazing thing happened. I stopped and I thought, You *are* doing it. There I was climbing this humongous tree, and I wasn't getting dizzy or nauseous or anything. It's true my palms were sweating like crazy and my heart was racing, but I figured those were the kinds of things that would happen to anybody under the circumstances.

Then I heard Ben's voice, soft and nearby. "Here, I'm here."

I wedged myself between a couple of branches and shined my flashlight on the branches above me. There he was, just a few feet away. Tears were running down his cheeks, but he smiled when he saw me.

"I knew you'd save me," he said.

And you know something? I did.

It took me about ten minutes to get him out of there, and it turned out to be a lot harder going *down* a tree in the dark than it was going up, but it helped that there were two of us. When we finally got to the bottom, Mrs. Coburn threw her arms around Ben—and Kelly threw her arms around me. It caught me by surprise, and I was too weak to resist.

As if I would have resisted anyway.

When we got back to Ben's house, Kelly was a lot cooler toward me, though. The two of us sat silently watching Ben eat half a pizza while his mother and my mother drank tea and went on about how nervous they'd been and what a hero I was and how even the 911 crew couldn't believe I'd gotten him out of that tree single-handedly.

I would have felt a lot better about being a hero if Kelly wasn't giving me the cold shoulder—and if Ben didn't keep sneaking these looks at me. "Okay," his eyes seemed to be saying, "maybe you got me out of that tree, but you were the reason I was up there in the first place."

Talk about guilt.

"If you kids will excuse me," Mrs. Coburn said, after she was sure Ben had had enough to eat, "I'd like to take a cup of hot tea and a cold compress and collapse in the living room."

"I'll join you," my mother said.

Which left me alone with Kelly and Ben.

We kept glancing at one another, waiting for someone to speak. I figured it was probably up to me.

When Ben picked up his plate and carried it to the sink, I said, "Where are you going?"

"No place," he answered with a shrug.

"Me, either," I said.

Out of the corner of my eye, I noticed Kelly smile. Just a little.

"Huh?" Ben said.

"Look, Ben, I think I know why you ran away."

"No, you don't."

"Maybe I do," I said. "And I just want you to know I'm not going anywhere, okay? Unless you want me to."

He stood there staring at me, then turned to rinse his plate in the sink. "Well," he said, his back to me, "now that you know how to climb trees, you might be more fun to have around." Then he turned to face me. "I guess you can stay," he said.

"All *right!*" I said. I motioned for him to come over and slapped him five. And then before he could get away, I gave him a hug. I hadn't planned to; it just sort of happened. Once it did, I held on tight. And so did Ben.

"Who wants ice cream?" Ben said, working his way out of my grip and wiping his nose as he crossed to the refrigerator.

"I do," I said.

"Me, too," said Kelly.

I looked at her and thought, This is going to be even harder than climbing that tree.

"Kelly," I said, "I need some advice." Her eyes flared up, but before she could get a word out, I went on. "There's this girl, okay? She's really terrific, but I've been too blind or stupid or . . ."

"Or both," Ben said, scooping out ice cream.

"Right," I said. Ben was catching on faster than Kelly. "See, I thought I wanted this *other* girl because I knew she was the kind of girl Mitch Buckley would want. And I just had to beat Mitch so bad that all I could think about was this girl. But meanwhile I was making a real mess of things with this other girl and—"

Kelly was smiling. "There are so many girls in this story," she said. "Which one are we talking about now?"

"The terrific one," I said. "The one who's been a real friend. So what I need to know is, how do I let this terrific girl know I'm sorry I messed things up and that . . . that I really like her?"

"It's like I told you before, Nick. Be yourself. Talk to the girl."

I took a deep breath. "Kelly," I said, "I'm sorry. I *have* been a jerk."

"Yep," Kelly said.

"Yep," Ben echoed, putting a bowl of ice cream down in front of me.

"Thanks for the support, guys," I said.

Ben shrugged. "What're friends for?"

"I guess I always thought talking to girls had to be hard," I told Kelly, "and it was so easy talking to you, well, I never noticed how much I liked you."

"I like you, too," Kelly said.

We sat there for a minute, not knowing what else to say. Ben looked back and forth between us.

"I now pronounce you husband and wife," he said at last. "You may kiss the bride."

Well, I didn't kiss anybody—not then, anyway— but I did ask Kelly to go to the dance with me, even if it was supposed to be girl-ask-boy, and she said yes.

Let me tell you something, I don't know what it would have been like to walk into that dance with Jennifer on my arm, but it couldn't have been any bet- ter than the way I felt with Kelly. And the funny thing was that the minute I saw Jennifer I wondered why I'd ever thought she was so beautiful in the first place. I mean, Kelly's like a million times better looking. At least, I think so.

Naturally, Jennifer was there with Mitch. And, boy, did she let me have it when she saw me.

"I can't believe you had the nerve to show up," she said, "after what you did to me."

"After what I did to you? You know, Jennifer, I don't think you ever wanted to go with me to this dance. So why did you ask me?"

By now, we had been joined by Lucas and Michelle and Augie and Lindsay. Lindsay was wearing the same dress as Jennifer, giving, I was pretty sure, the kiss of death to *that* friendship.

"Yeah," Lucas said, "why did you ask Nick?"

Jennifer looked around uncomfortably. "Well . . ."

"What difference does it make?" Mitch said, the white knight charging in to rescue his damsel in distress. "The bottom line, Nicky, old boy, is that she came with me. So it looks like you'll be wearing that tutu after all."

"No way, Mitchy, old chap," I said. "She asked me first."

"What are you two talking about?" Jennifer asked. "What tutu?"

Mitch and I glared at each other, our final showdown.

"Mitch and I made a little bet," I said.

"A bet about *me*?" Jennifer asked.

"Uh, yeah," Mitch mumbled. "We each bet that we would be the one you'd ask to the dance."

"I can't believe this," Jennifer said.

"I know," said Michelle, "isn't it disgusting?"

Kelly gave Jennifer a sympathetic look. "I couldn't believe it, either. It's so—"

"Sweet," Jennifer said. "Why, I think it's just the sweetest thing I ever heard."

No one knew what to say. At that moment, all I could do was look at Jennifer and Mitch and think: These two are made for each other.

As it turned out, we declared the bet a draw. Jennifer *had* asked both of us to the dance, even if she'd ended up going with Mitch. So neither of us had to put on a tutu and do that little dance.

I found out later that the reason Jennifer had taken so long to ask Mitch to the Vice-Versa Dance was that one of her rules about boys is that they have to ask *her* out first. She was just waiting for Mitch to ask her out on *one* date. If he had, she would have asked him to go with her to the dance. What happened at the mall was that he was just about to ask her to go to the movies when he saw me watching and chickened out. She got so mad that she told him she would ask the next boy from school that she saw. And we know who *that* was. So much for the miracle at the mall.

I also found out that Jennifer set me up that time at Alyssa's house. In fact, she was hiding under the table at the pizza place when Alyssa and I had come in. It seems that when Alyssa spilled the cup of soda, she'd soaked Jennifer. Serves her right, I'd say. Anyway, that's why Mitch was pushing us out of there. And why we got a free pizza.

You probably had that one figured out a long time ago.

I guess I was a little dumb when it came to Jennifer. I mean, I should have known right off that she couldn't have cared less about sensitive guys—or baby-sitting. She only took that class because she thought it would be an easy A. The joke was on her. Ms. Marlowe is making her repeat the class next semester.

But you know what? I don't spend my time worrying about Jennifer anymore. I've got more important things to do than try to impress her or beat Mitch. Like right now I've got a birthday party to go to. Ben is turning eight. I got him a dinosaur kit. It's a tyrannosaurus with about a million pieces. Hey, it'll probably take us the rest of the year to put it together, but that's fine by me.

I kind of like this baby-sitting thing. In fact, I'm sitting for Alyssa on Saturday night. Like Mitch said, I'm expanding my empire. Kelly tells me that's okay as long as I leave time for her. I told her not to worry.

Listen, I've got to go or I'll be late for that party—
and I still have to wake up my left foot. Pooch has
been lying on it for the last hour. I guess I could have
made him move, but he looked so comfortable there,
and like I always say, with a devoted pet like Pooch,
you make sacrifices.

This is what I think: Sometimes you put up with
stuff in life and sometimes you don't. It's all up to you.